STARK
REALISM

"You've read the book," Kelp said. "Well, uh, what did you think of it?"

"I thought it was pretty good," Dortmunder said.

Kelp grinned with relief. Clapping his hands together he said, "That's right. It *is* pretty good, isn't it? And you know what else it is?"

None of them knew.

"It's full of *detail*," Kelp said.

They all nodded. Dortmunder said, "But where do we come in?"

A sudden rush of excitement carried Kelp along on its crest. Crouching like a surfer in the curl, he leaned toward his audience and said, "Don't you see? That goddam book's a *blueprint*, a step-by-step *master plan!* All we do is *follow* it! *They* got away with it in the book, and *we'll* get away with it right here!"

They were staring.
stared back, fired wit
"Don't you see? We o
We *do* the book!"

JIMMY
THE KID

Also by Donald E. Westlake

Published by
THE MYSTERIOUS PRESS   *forthcoming

JIMMY THE KID

DONALD E. WESTLAKE

THE MYSTERIOUS PRESS

New York • London • Tokyo • Sweden

MYSTERIOUS PRESS EDITION

Copyright © 1974 by Donald E. Westlake
All rights reserved.

The Mysterious Press Edition is published by arrangement with the
author.

Cover art by Sonja Lamut and Nenad Jakesevic

Mysterious Press books are published in association with
Warner Books, Inc.
666 Fifth Avenue
New York, N.Y. 10103
A Warner Communications Company

Printed in the United States of America

First Mysterious Press Printing: June, 1989

10 9 8 7 6 5 4 3 2 1

This is for Henry Morrison,
who not only made it possible,
he made it necessary.

1

DORTMUNDER, WEARING BLACK and carrying his canvas bag of burglar tools, walked across the rooftops from the parking garage on the corner. At the sixth roof, he looked over the front edge to be absolutely sure he was on the right building, and felt dizzy for just a second when he saw the distant street six storeys down, floating like a ship in the glare of streetlights. Cars were parked along both sides, leaving one black lane open in the middle. A cab was going by down there, its yellow top glinting in the light. Behind the cab came a slow-moving police car; the unlit flasher dome on its roof looked like a piece of candy.

And this was the right place. The furrier's hanging sign was visible down there, right where it was supposed to be. Dortmunder, feeling a trifle queasy about the height, leaned back from the edge, carefully turned, and walked across the roof to the opposite side, where a fire escape led down into less dizzying darkness. The building backs were crammed so close together here that Dortmunder felt he could almost reach out and touch the grimy brick wall across the way, but all of the windows along here were dark. It was three o'clock in the morning, so no one was up and about.

Dortmunder went slowly down the fire escape. The canvas bag made muffled clanking sounds whenever it hit the fire escape railing, and he grimaced and clenched his teeth at every noise. Some of the windows he was passing belonged to storage lofts and other commercial enterprises, but some were apartments, this being the kind of Manhattan neighbourhood where families and factories live side by side. He didn't want anybody to wake up, mistake him for a peeping tom, and shoot him.

7

Second floor. A scarred metal door, painted black, led out to the fire escape, which stopped at this level. A metal ladder could be lowered for the last flight down, but Dortmunder didn't want the first-floor shop, he wanted the second-floor storage room. In almost total darkness, he put down the canvas bag, felt the door all over with his fingertips, and decided it would have to be a simple peeling operation. Noisy for a few seconds, but that couldn't be helped.

Kneeling, he zipped open his bag and got the right tools out by sense of touch. The chisel. The small crowbar. The large screwdriver with the rubber handle.

"Ssiss! "

He paused. He looked around and saw nothing but the darkness. It had sounded like somebody hissing at him.

Probably a rat in a garbage can. Dortmunder stood, and prepared to wedge the chisel in at the top corner of the door.

"Ssiss!"

By God, that almost sounded human. Dortmunder, feeling the hair starting to stand up on the back of his neck, clutched the chisel like a weapon and looked around some more.

"Ssiss! *Dort*-munder! "

He almost dropped the chisel. The hisser had hissed his name, a sibilant whisper that made the name *Dortmunder* sound as though it were full of *ess*es. Here in the darkness, with nobody around, somebody—some *thing*—was hissing his name.

My guardian angel, he thought. But no; if he *had* a guardian angel, it would have given up on him years ago.

It's Satan, he thought, he's come to get me. The hand holding the chisel trembled, and the chisel made little skittery rapping noises against the metal door.

"Dortmunder, up *here*! "

Up? Would Satan be above him? Wouldn't the devil be underneath? Blinking uncontrollably, Dortmunder

8

looked up. Above him, the grillwork lines of the fire escape stood out dimly against the dull red light that New York City always casts up to its cloud cover at night. Something, some creature, was on the fire escape, one level above him, silhouetted vaguely against the red sky, looming over him like a gargoyle on a church roof.

"Jesus! " Dortmunder whispered.

"Dortmunder," the creature hissed at him, "it's *me*! Kelp! "

"Oh, Jesus *Christ*! " Dortmunder said, and got so mad he forgot where he was and threw the chisel down. The clang it made when it hit the fire escape made him jump a foot.

"For Pete's sake, Dortmunder," Kelp whispered, "don't be so *noisy*! "

"Go away, Kelp," Dortmunder said. He spoke in a normal tone of voice, not giving a damn about anything any more.

"I want to talk to you," Kelp whispered. "May told me where you were."

"May has a big mouth," Dortmunder said, still speaking aloud.

"So do you, fella! " a voice shouted from one or two buildings away. "How about turning it off so we can get some sleep! "

Kelp whispered, "Come up here, Dortmunder, I want to talk to you."

"I don't want to talk to *you*," Dortmunder said. He wasn't keeping his voice down at all; in fact, it was starting to go up. "I don't *ever* want to talk to you," he said. "I don't even want to *see* you."

"How would you like to see some *cops*! " the voice yelled.

"Oh, shut up! " Dortmunder yelled back.

"We'll see about that! "

Somewhere, a window slammed.

Urgent, shrill, Kelp whispered, "Dortmunder, come up

9

here, will you? And keep it low, you're gonna get us in trouble."

Not keeping it low, Dortmunder said, "I'm not going up there, you're going away. I'm going to stay down here and do my work."

"You're on the wrong *floor*," Kelp whispered.

Dortmunder, bending down and feeling around for his chisel, frowned and looked up at the vague figure against the grey-red clouds. "I am not," he said.

"It's—there's an extra—that's the *basement* down there."

"The what?" Dortmunder's hand found the chisel. He straightened, holding it, and frowned down into impenetrable darkness. There *was* another storey down there, he was sure of it. So this was the second floor.

But Kelp whispered, "Why do you think I'm waiting up *here*? Count down from the roof if you don't believe me. You're gonna break into the *store*."

"I'm just in the same block with you," Dortmunder said, "and things get screwed up."

A light went on in a window, off to the left. Kelp, more urgently, whispered, "Come *up* here! You want to get *caught*?"

"Okay, fella," the voice shouted, "you asked for it. The cops are on the way."

Another voice yelled, "Why don't you people shut up?"

The first voice yelled, "It isn't me! It's those other clowns!"

"You got the biggest voice *I* can hear!" shouted voice number two.

"How would you like to go screw yourself?" voice number one wanted to know.

Another yellow window appeared. A third voice yelled, "How would the *two* of you like to go drown yourselves?"

"Dortmunder," Kelp whispered. "Come on, come on."

Voice number two was making a suggestion to voice number three. Voice number one was yelling to somebody

10

named Mary to call the cops again. A voice number four entered the chorus, and two more windows sprang out of the darkness. It was getting very bright back here.

Dortmunder, grumbling, muttering, annoyed into futile silence, went down on one knee and stolidly repacked his canvas bag. "A simple burglary," he told himself. "Kelp shows up. Can't even do a simple burglary." Around him the neighbourhood argument raged. People in pyjamas were leaning out of windows, shaking their fists at one another. Dortmunder zipped up the bag and got to his feet. "A simple quiet little peaceful job," he muttered. "*Kelp* shows up." Carrying the bag, he started back up the fire escape.

Kelp was waiting, one flight up. There was another black metal door there, standing open, and Kelp made hostlike gestures for Dortmunder to go in, but Dortmunder ignored him and went right on by. Going past, he caught a glimpse of furs hanging on racks inside there; so he really had been on the wrong floor. That didn't improve his disposition.

Kelp said, "Where you going?" There wasn't any point in whispering now, not with everybody else in the neighborhood shouting at once, so Kelp spoke in an ordinary voice.

Dortmunder didn't answer. He went on up the fire escape. He became aware after half a flight that Kelp was following him, and he considered turning around and telling him to go away, or possibly turning around and hitting Kelp on the head with the canvas bag, but he didn't do it. He didn't have the strength, he didn't have a positive enough attitude. He was feeling defeatist again, the way he always did around Kelp. So he just kept plodding up the fire escape stairs to the roof.

At the top he turned left and headed across the roofs toward the parking garage. He knew Kelp was trotting after him, but he tried to ignore the fact. He also tried to ignore it when Kelp caught up with him and walked next to him, panting and saying, "Don't go so fast, will ya?"

Dortmunder went faster.

"You were going in the wrong floor," Kelp said. "Is that *my* fault? I got there ahead of you, I jimmied the door, I thought I'd help."

"Don't help," Dortmunder said. "That's all I ask, don't help."

"If you'd stopped at the right floor," Kelp said, "I wouldn't have had to call you. We could have talked inside. I could have helped you carry the furs."

"Don't help," Dortmunder said.

"You went to the wrong *floor*."

Dortmunder stopped. He was one roof shy of the parking garage. He turned and looked at Kelp and said, "All right. One question. You've got a caper? You want me in on it?"

Kelp hesitated. It could be seen that he'd had a different plan in mind for broaching his subject, a method more circuitous and subtle. But it wasn't to be, and Dortmunder watched Kelp gradually accept the fact. Kelp sighed. "Yes," he said.

"The answer is no," Dortmunder said. He turned and headed again for the parking garage.

Hurrying after him, Kelp protested, "Why? You can't even *listen*?"

Dortmunder stopped again, and Kelp ran into him. Kelp was shorter than Dortmunder, and his nose ran into Dortmunder's shoulder. "Ow!" he said.

"I'll tell you why," Dortmunder said.

Kelp pressed a hand to his nose. "That hurt," he said.

"I'm sorry," Dortmunder said. "The last time I listened to you, I wound up running all over Long Island with a stolen bank, and what did I get out of it? A head cold."

"I think I've got a nosebleed," Kelp said. He was tenderly touching his nose with his fingertips.

"I'm sorry," Dortmunder said. "And the time before that, you remember what that was? That other time I listened to you? That goddam Balabomo Emerald, remember *that* one?"

"If you're blaming me for any of that," Kelp said, talking nasally because he was holding his nose, "I think it's very unfair."

"If I'm unfair," Dortmunder pointed out, "you don't want to be around me." And he turned away again and walked on.

Kelp trailed along, touching his nose and loudly sniffing. The two of them crossed to the last roof, and Dortmunder opened the door leading to the stairs. He went down, followed by Kelp, to an open, concrete-floored area with half a dozen dusty cars parked in it. Walking across the floor, with Kelp still behind him, he went down a concrete ramp past another parking level with more dusty cars, and at the third level down walked out past a lot of less dusty cars to a brown Volkswagen Microbus with red side curtains. Kelp, still talking nasally, said, "Where'd you get that?"

"I stole it," Dortmunder said. "Because you weren't around, nothing went wrong. I figured to be filling it with furs right now."

"That's not my fault," Kelp said. "You were on the wrong floor."

"It was because you were around," Dortmunder told him. "You're my jinx, I don't even have to know you're there and you screw me up."

"That isn't fair, Dortmunder," Kelp said. "Now, you know that." He gestured with both hands.

"You're bleeding on your shirt," Dortmunder told him.

"Oh, *damn*." Kelp closed his fingers over his nose again. "Listen," he twanged, "lemme just tell you about this thing."

"If I listen to you—" Dortmunder started, and then stopped and shook his head. Sometimes there just wasn't anything to be done with a bad hand but play it. He knew that, if anybody did. "Screw it," he said. "Get in the car."

13

Behind the hand holding his nose, Kelp beamed. "You won't regret this, Dortmunder," he said, and ran around to the other side of the Microbus.

"I regret it already," Dortmunder said. But he got into the Microbus and started the engine and drove it down and out of the garage. A man in a green work shirt and green work pants sitting on a kitchen chair out on the sidewalk did not look up as they went by. Kelp, looking out at that man, said, "Isn't he the garage man?"

"Yes."

"How come you can just drive in and out?"

"Twenty dollars," Dortmunder said. His expression was grim. "That's something else you cost me," he said.

"Aw, now, Dortmunder, you're just in a bad mood."

"No kidding."

"Tomorrow you'll think it over," Kelp said, "you'll realize it isn't right to blame me for everything."

"I don't blame you for everything," Dortmunder said. "I don't blame you for the Second World War and I don't blame you for the Johnstown flood. But everything else I *do* blame you for."

"Tomorrow you'll feel different," Kelp said.

Dortmunder glanced at him, to give him an unbelieving look, and said, "You're bleeding on yourself again."

"Oh." Kelp put his head back, and stared at the Volkswagen's roof.

"You might as well tell me the caper," Dortmunder said, "so I can say no and get it over with."

"It's not like that," Kelp said, holding his nose and talking to the roof. "I got nothing to *tell* you exactly. It's more to *show* you."

Like the emerald. "Where is it?"

With the hand that wasn't holding his nose, Kelp reached into his jacket pocket and pulled out a paperback book. "It's this," he said.

Dortmunder was approaching an intersection with a green light. He made his turn, drove a block, and stopped at a red light. Then he looked at the book Kelp was waving. He said, "What's that?"

"It's a book."

"I know it's a book. What is it?"

"It's for you to read," Kelp said. "Here, take it." He was still staring at the roof and holding his nose, and he was merely waving the book in Dortmunder's direction.

So Dortmunder took the book. The title was *Child Heist*, and the author was somebody named Richard Stark. "Sounds like crap," Dortmunder said.

"Just read it," Kelp said.

"Why?"

"Read it. Then we'll talk."

Dortmunder hefted the book in his hand. A skinny paperback. "I don't get the point," he said.

"I don't want to say anything till after you read it," Kelp said. "Okay? I mean, after all, you gave me a nosebleed, you can anyway read a book."

Dortmunder thought of saying several things about furs, but he didn't. The traffic light was green. "Maybe," he said, and tossed the paperback behind him, and drove on.

2

STAN MURCH MADE his call from a diner pay phone. "Maximilian's Used Cars, Miss Caroline speaking."

"Hi, Harriet. Max there?"

"To whom am I speaking, please?"

"This is Stan."

"Oh, hi, Stan. One moment, please, Max is explaining the guarantee to a dissatisfied customer."

"Sure," Murch said. The phone booth was inside the diner, but it had a window that overlooked the blacktop parking lot, and Jericho Turnpike beyond. A dozen cars winkled in the thin October sunlight. The car Stan had in mind, an almost-new white Continental, a definite cream-puff, was parked almost in front of him. The driver had staggered in just a few minutes ago, drunk out of his mind even though it was barely two o'clock in the afternoon, and was now sprawled in a booth in the rear of the diner, occa-- sionally spilling black coffee on himself. All things considered, Murch told himself, I'm doing that bird a favour. He shouldn't be driving in his condition.

"Yah?"

Murch, who had been leaning against the side of the booth and brooding at the Continental, now stood upright and said, "Max?"

"Yah. Stan?"

"Sure. Listen, Max, you still interested in good recent acquisitions?"

"You mean where I got to do my own paper?"

"That's the kind."

"That's a little tricky, Stan. Depends on the vee-hickle."

"A creampuff white Continental. Like new."

"You're reading me my ad out of *Newsday*."

"What do you think, Max?"

"Bring it over, we'll have a look."

"Right," Murch said, and was about to hang up when another vehicle made the turn from Jericho Turnpike into the diner's parking lot. It was a car carrier, with four Buick Rivieras on it: a powder blue, a maroon, and two bronzes. "Wait a second," Murch said.

"Hah?"

"Just hold on."

The car carrier growled up to the diner, puffing diesel exhaust out of a pipe at the top of the cab, and came at last to a shuddering stop. The driver, a stout fellow in a brown leather jacket, climbed down to the blacktop as though both his legs had fallen asleep, and then stood there yawning and scratching his crotch.

"Stan? You there?"

"Wait a second," Murch said. "Just a second."

The driver, done with his yawning and scratching, walked over to the diner entrance, leaving Murch's sight for a few seconds. Murch turned around and looked through the phone booth's interior window. He watched the car carrier driver amble across to the rear part of the diner and sit in the next booth to the sprawled driver of the Continental. Neither of them could see the parking lot from where they were.

"Stan?"

"Listen, Max," Murch said. "You interested in more, maybe? Other cars, maybe?"

"I'm always interested in top quality, Stan, you know that."

"See you soon," Murch said. Hanging up, he left the booth and the diner and strolled over to the car carrier. About to climb up into the cab, he glanced over at the Continental, sorry to have to leave it behind. Oh, well, four was better than one.

Or . . .

Hmmmm. Murch moved away from the cab and considered the entire length of the car carrier. It was made to carry six automobiles, three on top and three on the bottom, but it only had two in each part. The rear spaces were unoccupied, top and bottom.

Hmmmmm. Murch walked around to the rear of the vehicle and considered it carefully. A kind of heavy metal tailgate was up across the back, with looped chains at both ends. Wouldn't that tailgate double as a ramp if it were lowered?

Murch moved closer, studying the tailgate's operation. Opening those two hooks should release the thing, then one should pay out his chain through that ratchet, and. . . .

Might as well try it. He released the hooks, he grasped the chain, he began to feed it slowly through the ratchet. The tailgate lowered itself. Murch fed the chain faster, and

17

the tailgate lowered faster. *Tonk*, the tailgate went against the blacktop. It was now a ramp.

Fine. Leaving the car carrier, Murch walked briskly but not too hurriedly across the lot to the Continental. He had his bunch of keys in his hand when he got there, but the Continental's door was unlocked. He slid behind the wheel, tried three keys, and started the engine with the fourth. There was a strong smell of bourbon inside the car.

Murch put it in reverse, backed the Continental around in a loop, switched to drive, and steered across the parking lot and up the ramp and into the car carrier. He switched off the engine, set the hand brake, and got out of the car. He climbed through the metal struts of the side, attained the blacktop, and quickly raised the tailgate again. There wasn't any way to chain the Continental in place, the way the Buicks were chained, but he'd be taking it easy. He also didn't have that far to go.

Key number two started the car carrier engine. Murch turned the big flat wheel, the car carrier lumbered forward, and slowly he made his getaway out onto Jericho Turnpike.

It took twenty-five minutes to drive to Maximilian's Used Cars. When he got there, Murch took the side street next to the car lot, then turned in at the anonymous driveway behind it. He stopped amid tall weeds and the white clapboard backs of garages, climbed down out of the cab, and went through an unlocked gate in a chain-link fence. A path through weeds and shrubbery led him to the rear of Maximilian's office structure, a California-looking thing in pink stucco. He opened a door, went through into a grey-panelled office, and heard Max in the next room saying, "What you got to read in the guarantee is every word."

A very angry male voice said, loudly, "If you read every *word* of that guarantee, you don't guarantee *anything*!"

"That's how you say," Max said.

Murch opened the connecting door, and stuck his head

in. The customer was big and muscular, but intellectually out of his depth. He had the bewildered look of a swimmer who hadn't known there were whirlpools anywhere around here. Murch, ignoring him, said to Max, "Max, could I interrupt?"

"I hope so," Max said. A big old man with heavy jowls and thin white hair, he always wore a dark vest, wide open, and no tie. His white shirt was usually smudged from leaning against used cars. Now, getting to his feet from behind his desk, he said to the customer, "Read a little. Read the words. I'll be back."

"You better be," the customer said, but there wasn't any real threat in it. He was buffaloed, and he was himself beginning to understand it.

Max and Murch crossed the empty office and went out the rear door. Murch said, "That the same customer as when I called?"

"Some of them just won't go away," Max said. "Don't they have homes? Some friend of yours called. On the telephone. You shouldn't go away without him coming here."

"Who?"

"A little name," Max said, as they followed the path toward the chain-link fence. "Chip? Shep?"

"Kelp?"

"If you say so," Max said, and they stepped out onto the driveway, now filled with the bulk of the car carrier. Max looked at it. "Jesus, Mary and Joseph," he said. "You stealing now in bunches? They ain't *grapes*! "

"It was there," Murch said. "I put the Continental on the back."

Max went down along the side of the car carrier, looking at the automobiles in there. "In broad daylight," he said. "*You* go talk to the customer."

Murch shook his head. "I don't talk to customers," he said. "What I do, I drive."

"So I see." Max looked at the cars and the car carrier. "I'll take them," he said.

19

"Fine."

"Come around next week, we'll talk money."

"Okay."

Max pointed down the driveway. "You'll put them around by the body shop," he said.

"Have your people do it," Murch said. "I'd rather not stick around."

"What about the truck?"

Murch frowned at the truck. "What about it?"

"*I* don't want it," Max said. "You read the sign out front, it says used *cars*. I got no use for a truck."

"Neither do I, Max."

"Take it back where you got it."

"I don't want to drive it any more."

"You can't dump a stolen truck on me, Stanley, that isn't a thing to do."

"Take it someplace else tonight," Murch told him. "Just park it out along the road. Have one of your people do it."

"Why not keep it?" Max suggested. "You could drive around in it, every time you see a nice car just toss it in."

Murch looked at the truck, considering the idea. It had a certain appeal. But finally he shook his head and said, "No, it wouldn't be any good. Too noticeable."

"Stan, if I got to unload this truck, it's got to cost you."

"Sure, Max, we'll take ten bucks off." Murch shrugged it away, and turned to go back to the used-car lot. Behind him, Max looked at the car carrier the way the dissatisfied customer had looked at Max. Then he shook his head, and followed Murch through the chain-link fence.

The customer wasn't in the office. "Now what?" Max said. "I'll tell you, he's out front breaking windshields. We had one just last spring, came in, complained about all that stuff they always complain about, and first thing you know he's got a wrench, he's breaking windshields right and left. Terrible."

"Terrible," Murch agreed.

The two of them walked out the front door. Used cars

were lined up on three sides of them, with placards in their windshields. Max pointed. "There he is! And who's that with him?"

"That's my friend Kelp," Murch said.

Kelp and the customer were standing next to a dilapidated green Chevrolet. They were talking. The customer seemed less aggrieved than before. In fact, he chuckled at something Kelp said, and he didn't seem to mind it when Kelp patted his arm.

"Ho ho," Max said. He looked and sounded awed.

Kelp and the customer shook hands. The customer got into the green Chevrolet and started the engine. It sounded awful. Kelp waved to him and the customer waved back and drove off. Something under the car was scraping, causing an even worse noise than the engine and also causing sparks. The Chevrolet jounced down the driveway and went away.

Kelp came walking over, a cheerful smile on his face in the sunshine. "Hi, Stan," he said.

"Mister Chelp," Max said, "could you use a job?"

"What? No, thanks, I've got something on the fire."

Murch said, "You wanted to talk to me?"

"Right. You want a lift somewhere?"

"I left my car at a diner on Jericho Turnpike."

"I'll take you there," Kelp said.

Murch said so long to Max, who was still looking dazed, and went with Kelp to the car he had parked at the curb. It was a Mercedes, with MD plates. Murch said, "Still copping doctors' cars, huh?"

"They got the best taste," Kelp said. "Power steering, power seats, power everything. You never catch a doctor cranking his own window down. Get in."

They got into the car, Murch pushing a paperback that was resting on the seat out of his way. Kelp started the engine, and they rolled away from the curb.

Murch said, "What's the story?"

21

Kelp, pointing to the book on the seat between them, said. "That."

Murch laughed politely.

"No, on the level," Kelp said. "What I want you to do, I want you to read that book."

"Read a *book*?" Murch read the *Daily News* and several car magazines, but he didn't read *books*.

"You'll like it," Kelp told him. "And I've got an idea that hooks up with it."

Murch picked up the book. He would like it? *Child Heist*, by Richard Stark. "What's it about?"

"About a crook," Kelp said. "A crook named Parker. He'll remind you of Dortmunder."

"That sounds great," Murch said, but without much enthusiasm. He riffled through the book: words on every page.

"You read it," Kelp said. "Dortmunder's reading it, too. And have your Mom read it. Then when everybody's had a chance to go through the book, we'll have a meeting."

"Dortmunder's in on this?"

"Sure," Kelp said, casual and convincing.

Murch opened the book, feeling the stirrings of curiosity.

CHAPTER ONE

When the guard came to open the cell door, Parker said to the big man named Krauss, "Come see me next week when you get out. I think I'll have something on."

3

KELP WAS VERY excited and very happy. He couldn't sit in one place, and the result was he got to Dortmunder and May's place half an hour early for the meeting. He didn't want to risk annoying Dortmunder again, so he spent the half hour walking around the block.

He was so sure of this idea that he didn't see any possible way for Dortmunder to turn it down. With Dortmunder and May in, plus Murch to do the driving and Murch's Mom to handle the kid, it was all going to work just beautifully. Just like the book.

The way Kelp had come across that book, he'd been in jail at the time: a fact he didn't intend to mention to anybody. It had been upstate in Rockland County, a small town where he'd run into a little trouble when some cops stopping cars to look for drugs had found a whole lot of burglar tools in his trunk. It had taken five days to get the whole thing squashed because of the element of illegal search, but during those five days Kelp had been kept locked up in the local pokey. And a very poky pokey it had been, too—nothing to do but roll Bugler cigarettes and read paperback books donated by some local ladies' club.

Several of the books had been by this writer Richard Stark, always about the same crook, named Parker. Robbery stories, big capers, armoured cars, banks, all that sort of thing. And what Kelp really liked about the books was that Parker always got away with it. Robbery stories where the crooks didn't get caught at the end—fantastic. For Kelp, it was like being an American Indian and going to a western movie where the cowboys lose. Wagon train wiped out, cavalry lost in the desert, settlement abandoned,

23

ranchers and farmers driven back across the Mississippi. Grand.

Child Heist was the third of the Parker novels he'd read, and even while he was reading it he'd known it meant something special to him, even more than the others. And as he was finishing the book the revelation had come on him like a sudden flood of heavenly light, like his little grey cell had just been illumined by a thousand suns. That's the way it had been. And when, the next day, the Public Defender had finally gotten him sprung, he'd walked out of there with *Child Heist* concealed inside his shirt, and as soon as he'd made it back to the city he'd gone to a bookstore and picked up half a dozen more copies.

Would the others see it the way he had? May probably would, she was smart, and in any case she'd go along with it if Dortmunder did. Murch probably not, he tended not to understand anything that didn't have wheels, but that wouldn't really matter. Not if Dortmunder went for it. Murch would follow Dortmunder's lead, and Murch's Mom would follow Murch.

So it all came down to Dortmunder, and how could Dortmunder say no? It was a natural, it had struck Kelp in that jail cell as a natural, and it was going to strike Dortmunder as a natural. Going to. Have to. No question.

Kelp, growing more and more terrified that Dortmunder wasn't going to think it was a natural, walked around and around the block for half an hour until a voice called to him from amid the traffic, "Hey, Kelp!"

He looked up and saw a cab going by, with Murch in the back seat, waving at him out the window. Kelp waved back and the cab continued on, toward the building in the middle of the block where Dortmunder and May lived. Kelp turned around and walked briskly after it, and saw the cab pull in next to a fire hydrant down there. Murch got out, waving at Kelp again, and then the driver got out and walked around the front of the cab to the sidewalk.

The driver was short and stocky, wearing grey pants and a black leather jacket and a cloth cap.

"Hi," Kelp shouted, and waved.

Murch stood waiting, and when Kelp got there he said, "Hey, Kelp. How come you were going the wrong way?"

Kelp frowned at him. "The wrong way?"

"You were going that way. You miss the address?"

"Oh, right!" Kelp said. He didn't want to display nervousness or indecision, so he shouldn't mention about walking around the block for half an hour. "Ha ha," he said. "How do you like that, I walked right on by it. I guess I must have been thinking, huh?"

The cabdriver said, "We going in or what are we gonna do? I could be out making a buck." She pulled the cloth cap off, and it was Murch's Mom.

"Oh, hi, Mrs. Murch," Kelp said. "I didn't recognize you. Sure, let's go in."

"This is my shift," Murch's Mom said. "I'm supposed to be working now."

"It'll be a short meeting, Mom," Murch said. "Then maybe you'll get somebody that wants to go to the airport."

The three of them had entered the tiny vestibule of the building, and Kelp was pressing the button for Dortmunder and May's apartment. Murch's Mom said, "You know the kind of fare I'll get? You know the way it's been lately? Park *Slope*, that's what I'll get, into darkest Brooklyn for a two-bit tip and no customers and drive back to Manhattan empty. *That's* what I get."

The door buzzed and Kelp pushed it open. He said, "Mrs. Murch, your days of driving a taxicab are over."

"I've had traffic cops say the same thing." She really wasn't in a wonderful mood at all.

The staircase was narrow; they had to go up one at a time. Kelp let Murch's Mom go first, and naturally her son had to follow, so Kelp went up last. He called past Murch, "Did you read the book, Mrs. Murch?"

"I read it." She was stumping up the stairs as though stair-climbing was the punishment for a crime she hadn't committed.

"Wha'd you think?"

She shrugged. Grudging it, she said, "Make a nice movie."

"Make a nice *bundle*," Kelp told her.

Murch said, "The part where they put the car in the truck. That was okay."

Kelp was feeling the awkwardness of a guy bringing his new girl friend around to meet the fellas at the bowling alley. He called up the stairs to Murch's Mom's back, "I thought it had like a kind of realism to it."

She didn't say anything. Murch said, "And they got away with it at the end. That was okay."

"Right," Kelp said. All of a sudden he was convinced Dortmunder wasn't going to see it. Murch hadn't seen it, Murch's Mom hadn't seen it, and Dortmunder wasn't going to see it. And Dortmunder had this prejudice anyway about ideas brought to him by Kelp, even though none of the disasters of the past had been truly Kelp's fault.

They were at the third-floor landing, and May was standing in the open doorway of the apartment. There was a cigarette dangling in the corner of her mouth, and she was wearing a dark blue dress and a green cardigan sweater with the buttons open and with a pocket down by the waist that was bulged out of shape by a pack of cigarettes and two packs of matches. She looked very flat-footed, because she had on the white orthopaedic shoes she wore in her job as a cashier at a Bohack's supermarket. She was a tall thin woman with slightly greying black hair, and she was usually squinting because of cigarette smoke in her eyes, since at all times she kept a cigarette burning away in the corner of her mouth.

Now, she said hello to everybody and invited them in, and Kelp paused just inside the door to say, "Did you read it?"

26

Murch and his Mom had gone through the foyer into the living room. Voices could be heard in there, as they greeted Dortmunder. May, closing the front door, nodded and said, "I liked it."

"Good," Kelp said. He and May went into the living room, and Kelp watched Dortmunder just leaving the room by the opposite door. "Uh," Kelp said.

May said, "You want a beer?" She called after Dortmunder, "John, and a beer for Kelp."

"Oh," Kelp said. "He's getting beer."

Murch and his Mom were settling on the sofa. The two full ashtrays on the drum table suggested that May was probably claiming the blue armchair, and that left only the grey armchair. Dortmunder would be sitting in that.

"Have a seat," May said.

"No thanks," Kelp said. "I'd rather stand. I'm sort of up and excited, you know?"

Beer cans were being opened in the kitchen; kop, kop, kop. Murch's Mom said, "May, I'm crazy about that lamp. Where'd you get it?"

"Fortunoff's," May said. "On sale, a discontinued model."

Murch said, "I know we're a little late, but we ran into traffic on the Brooklyn-Queens Expressway. I couldn't figure it out."

"I *told* you there was construction there," his mother said. "But you don't listen to your mother."

"At eight o'clock at night? I figured four, five o'clock, they go home. Am I supposed to know they leave the machinery there, close the thing down to one lane all *night*?"

Kelp said, "To come to Manhattan you take the Brooklyn-Queens Expressway?"

"Up to the Midtown Tunnel," Murch said. "You see, coming from Canarsie—"

Dortmunder, coming in then with his hands full of beer cans, said, "Everybody can drink out of the can, right?"

27

They all agreed they could, and then Murch went on with his explanation to Kelp, "Coming up out of Canarsie," he said, "you've got special problems, see. There's different routes you can take that's better at different times of day. So what we did this time, we took Pennsylvania Avenue, but then we *didn't* take the Interborough. See what I mean? We took Bushwick Avenue instead, and crossed over to Broadway. Now, we *could* have taken the Williamsburg Bridge, but—"

"Which is exactly what we should have done," Murch's Mom said, and drank some beer.

"Now, that's what I'll do next time," Murch admitted. "Until they get all that machinery off the BQE. But usually the best way is the BQE up to the Midtown Tunnel, and *then* into Manhattan." He was leaning urgently toward Kelp, gesturing with his full beer can. "See what I mean?"

It was more of an explanation than Kelp had been looking for. "I see what you mean," he said.

Dortmunder handed Kelp a beer and gestured at the grey armchair. "Have a seat."

"No, thanks. I think I'd rather stand."

"Suit yourself," Dortmunder said, and went over to sit on the arm of May's chair. "Go ahead," he said.

All at once, Kelp had stage fright. All at once he'd lost all confidence in his idea and all confidence in his ability to put the idea across. "Well," he said, and looked around at the four waiting faces, "well. You've all read the book."

They all nodded.

The empty chair was like a bad omen. Kelp was standing there in front of everybody like an idiot, and right next to him was this empty chair. Turning his head slightly, trying not to see the empty chair, he said, "And I asked you all what you thought of it, and you all thought it was pretty good, right?"

Three of them nodded, but Dortmunder said, "You didn't ask me what I thought of it."

"Oh. That's right. Well, uh, what did you think of it?"

"I thought it was pretty good," Dortmunder said.

Kelp grinned with relief.. His natural optimism was returning to him now. Clapping his hands together he said, "That's right. It *is* pretty good, isn't it? And you know what else it is?"

None of them knew.

"It's full of *detail*," Kelp said. "The whole thing is worked out right from one end to the other, every detail. Isn't that right?"

They all nodded. Dortmunder said, "But where do *we* come in?"

Kelp hesitated; this was the moment. The grey armchair hung like a teardrop in his peripheral vision. "We do it!" he said.

They all looked at him. Murch's Mom said, irritably, "What was that?"

It was out now, and a sudden rush of excitement carried Kelp along on its crest. Crouching like a surfer in the curl, he leaned toward his audience and said, "Don't you see? That goddam book's a *blueprint*, a step-by-step *master plan!* All we do is *follow* it! *They* got away with it in the book, and *we'll* get away with it right here!"

They were staring at him openmouthed. He stared back, fired with the vision of his idea. "Don't you see? We do the caper in the book! We *do the book!*"

4

DORTMUNDER JUST SAT there. The others, as they began to catch hold of Kelp's idea, starting making exclamations, asking questions, making comments, but Dortmunder just sat there, heavily, and thought about it.

Murch said, "I get it. You mean we do everything they do in the book."

"That's right! "

May said, "But it's a book about a kidnapping. It isn't a robbery, it's a kidnapping."

"It works the same way," Kelp told her. "What difference does it make, it's still a caper, and every detail is laid right out there for us. How to pick the kid, how to get the kid, how to get the payoff—"

May said, "But you can't kidnap a little child! That's *mean*. I'm surprised at you."

Kelp said, "No, it isn't. We wouldn't *hurt* the kid. I mean, we wouldn't hurt him anyway, but they make a whole point about that in the book, how if they give the kid back unhurt the cops won't try so hard to get them later on. Wait, I'll find the place, I'll read it to you."

Kelp reached into his hip pocket and pulled out a copy of the book. Dortmunder watched him, saw him leafing through it looking for the place, and still didn't say anything. He just sat there and thought about it.

Dortmunder was not a natural reader, but his times inside prison walls had shown him the usefulness of reading when you're waiting for a certain number of days to go by. Reading can speed the days a little, and that's all to the good. So all in all it had been a fairly familiar experience for him, reading a book, though strange to be doing it in a place with no bars over the window. And also strange to be doing it for some other reason outside the act of reading itself. All the way through he had kept wondering what Kelp had in mind, had even distracted himself from the story here and there while trying to guess what the purpose of it all could be, and the truth had never occurred to him. A blueprint. Kelp wanted them to read the book because it was a blueprint.

Now Kelp was leafing back and forth through his copy, trying to find the part where it had said not to kill the child they were kidnapping. "I know it's here somewhere," he was saying.

"We all read it," Murch's Mom said. "Don't start recit-it to us, like some Traffic Court judge."

"Okay," Kelp said, and closed the book again. Standing there, holding it, looking like some kind of paperback preacher, he said, "You all agree with me, don't you? You see what a natural this is, what a *winner* this is."

"There's a lot of driving in it," Murch said. "I noticed that right away."

"Plenty for you to do," Kelp told him eagerly.

"And they got the roads right," Murch said. "I mean, the guy that wrote the book, he got all the roads right."

May said, "But you're still talking about kidnapping a child, and I still say that's a mean, terrible thing to do."

"Not if you do it like this book *says*."

Murch's Mom said, "I suppose you'd want May and me to take care of this brat, like the women in the book."

Kelp said, "Well, we're not talking about a baby or anything, you don't have to change anybody's diaper or anything like that. We're talking about a kid maybe ten, twelve years old."

"That's very sexist," Murch's Mom said.

Kelp looked blank. "Hah?"

"Wanting May and me to take care of the kid. Role-assumption. It's sexist."

"Goddammit, Mom," Murch said, "you've been off with those consciousness-raising ladies again."

"I drive a cab," she said. "I'm no different from a man."

Kelp said. "You want *me* to take care of the kid?" He seemed honestly bewildered.

Murch's Mom snorted. "What does a man know about taking care of a child?"

"But—"

"I just wanted you to know," she said. "It was sexist, and I wanted you to know it was sexist."

"And *I* still say it's mean," May said. Beside her, Dort-

31

munder took a deep breath, but he didn't say anything. He was watching Kelp, listening to everybody and thinking.

Kelp said to May, "How could it be mean? With you and Murch's Mom to take care of the kid, who's gonna treat him mean? We follow what the book says, he'll never be in any danger, and he won't even get scared. He'll probably be glad he doesn't have to go to school for a couple of days."

Dortmunder rose slowly to his feet. "Kelp," he said.

Kelp looked at him, alert, bright-eyed, eager to be of assistance.

"You and me," Dortmunder said, "we've worked together a few times over the years, am I right?"

Kelp said, "Now, you're not gonna start dredging up the past, blaming me for—"

"I'm not talking about blame," Dortmunder said. "I'm just saying we worked together."

"Well, sure," Kelp said. "That's right, sure, we're longtime partners."

"Now, Stan here," Dortmunder said, "he's worked with us, too. What his job is, he drives, am I right?"

"I'm the best," Murch said.

"That's right," Kelp said. He seemed a little confused, but still bright-eyed and eager to please. "Stan drives, and he's the best."

"And what do I do?" Dortmunder asked him.

"You?" Kelp moved his hands vaguely. "You know what you do," he said. "You run it."

"I run it. I make the plan, isn't that right?"

"Well, sure," Kelp said.

"Now," Dortmunder said, and his voice was beginning to rise just a little, "are you saying all those things that went wrong in the past are *my* fault?"

"What? No, no, I never—"

"You're going to bring in a *plan*?"

"But—"

32

"You don't like the way I do plans, is that it? You think there's something *wrong* with the plans I work out?"

"No, I—"

"You think some *book writer's* gonna do you a better plan than *I* am, is that what you come here to say?"

"Dortmun—"

"You can get right out of here," Dortmunder said, and pointed a big-knuckled finger at the door.

"Just let me—"

"You and that Richard Smart or whatever the hell his name is," Dortmunder raged, "the *two* of you can get the hell out of here, and don't come back! "

5

MAY HAD PUT together a special dinner, all of Dortmunder's favourites: Salisbury steak, steamed green beans, whipped potatoes from a mix, enriched white bread, beer in the can, and boysenberry Jell-O for dessert. On the table were lined up the ketchup, the A-1 sauce, the Worcestershire sauce, the salt and pepper and sugar, the margarine, and the can of evaporated milk. She had the entrée done by midnight, and put it in the oven to keep warm till Dortmunder got home at quarter to four.

From the slope of his shoulders when he walked in she knew things hadn't gone well. Maybe she should wait, and broach the subject some other time? No; if she waited for John Dortmunder to be in a good mood they'd both of them be very, very old before she ever said anything.

He dropped his bag of tools on the grey armchair, where they clanked. He unzipped his black jacket, peeled off his black gloves, shook his head, and said, "I don't know, May. I just don't know."

"Something go wrong?"

"Twenty-five minutes going through that door," Dortmunder said. "I did everything right, everything smooth and perfect. Not a sound, not a peep. I go in through the door, I flash the light around, you know what the place·is?"

She shook her head. "I can't imagine," she said.

"Empty."

"Empty?"

"Since last Tuesday and today," he said, waving one hand around, "they went out of business. Can you figure that? Just last Tuesday I walked by the front of the place, they're still open. All right, they're having an up-to-fifty-percent-off sale, but they're *open*. Who expects them to go out of business?"

"I guess times are bad all over," May said.

"I'd like to take the guy had that store," Dortmunder said, "and punch him right in the head."

"Well, it isn't his fault either," May said. "He probably feels just as bad about closing up as you do."

With a cynical look, Dortmunder shook his head and said, "Not damn likely. He made out on that sale he had there, don't you think he didn't. And what do *I* get? I get zip."

"There'll be other times," May said. She wished she knew how to console him. "Anyway, wash up and I've got a nice dinner for you."

Dortmunder nodded, heavy and fatalistic. Walking away toward the bathroom, shrugging out of his jacket, he muttered, "Living off the proceeds of a woman." He shook his head again.

May scrinched her face up. He was always using that phrase, whenever things went wrong, and it was perfectly true that when he didn't make any money they had to live on her salary and fringe benefits from Bohack's, but she didn't mind. She'd told him a hundred times that she didn't mind. All she minded, actually, was that phrase: "Living off the proceeds of a woman." Somehow, the impression that phrase gave her didn't seem to have anything to do with being a cashier at Bohack's.

Oh, well. He didn't mean anything bad by it. May padded on back to the kitchen to see to dinner, and also to change cigarettes. The one burning away in the corner of her mouth had become no bigger than an ember by now, causing a sensation of heat against her lips. She reached up, plucked the burning coal from her mouth with thumb and two fingers, and flipped it into the sink, where it sizzled in complaint and then died. Meanwhile, May had already taken the crumpled pack of Lucky Strikes from her sweater pocket and was finagling one cigarette out of it. It was a process like removing an accident victim from his crushed automobile. Freeing the cigarette, she straightened and smoothed it, and went looking for matches. Unlike most chain smokers, she couldn't light the new cigarette from the old, there never being enough of the old one left to hold onto, so she had a continuing supply problem with matches.

Like now, for instance. There were no matches at all in the kitchen. Rather than carry the hunt through the rest of the apartment she turned on a front burner of the gas stove, crouched down in front of it, and crept up on the flame like a peeping tom creeping up on an open window. The smell of cigarette smoke mingled in the air with the smell of singed eyebrow. Squinting her eyes shut, she ducked back, puffed, shook her head, wiped her eyes, turned off the burner, and saw to dinner.

Dortmunder was sitting at the table in the dinette end of the living room when she carried the two hot plates in, using potholders with cartoons on them. Dortmunder looked at the food as she put it before him, and he almost smiled. "Looks real nice," he said.

"I thought you'd like it." She sat down opposite him, and for a while they just ate together in companionable silence. She didn't want to rush into this conversation, and in fact she wasn't even sure how she would start it. All she knew was that she wasn't looking forward to it.

She waited till they were having their coffee and Jell-O, and then said, "I had a call today from Murch's Mom."

"Oh yeah?" He sounded neither interested nor suspicious. What a simple, honest, trusting man, May thought, looking at him, feeling for him again the same tenderness as when they'd first met, the time she caught him shoplifting in Bohack's. That time, he hadn't run or lied or complained or caused any trouble at all; he'd just stood there, looking so defeated she hadn't had the heart to turn him in. She'd even helped him stuff the sliced cheese and the packaged baloney back into his armpits, and had said, "Look, why not hit the Grand Union from now on?" And he'd said, "I always liked the Bohack coffee." It was the first thing he'd ever said to her.

She cleared her throat; she was feeling misty and emotional, and that would never do. Much as she hated the role, what she had to do now was start manipulating her man; it was, after all, for his own good. So she said, "She told me, Murch's Mom told me, that Andy Kelp is still trying to organize that kidnapping idea."

Dortmunder paused with a spoonful of Jell-O, gave a disgusted look, and went back to his eating.

"He wanted Stan to drive," May said, "but Stan wouldn't go into it without you."

"Good," Dortmunder said.

"I'm worried about Kelp," May said. "You know what he's like, John."

"He's a jinx," Dortmunder said. "He's also an ingrate, and besides that he's a bigmouth. Let's not spoil a nice dinner with talk about Kelp."

"I'm just afraid of the kind of woman he'll get," May said. "You know, to take care of the child."

Dortmunder frowned. "What child?"

"The one they kidnap."

Dortmunder shook his head. "He'll never get it off the

36

ground. Andy Kelp couldn't steal third in the Little League."

"Well, that would make it even worse," May said. "He's really determined to do it, you know. He'll get the wrong people, some awful woman who doesn't care about children, and some barfly to do the driving, and they'll just get themselves in trouble."

"Good," Dortmunder said.

"But what if the child gets hurt? What if the police surround the hideout, what if there's a shoot-out?"

"A shoot-out? With Kelp? He's so gun-shy, he goes out to the track, he surrenders at the beginning of every race."

"But what about the other people with him? There's no telling *who* he'll wind up with."

Dortmunder looked pained, and May remembered that he and Kelp really were old friends; so maybe there was a chance, after all. But then Dortmunder's expression became mulish, and he said, "Just so he doesn't wind up with me. He's jinxed me long enough."

May cast around for another argument, considered a specific mention of the friendship between Dortmunder and Kelp, and finally decided not to do that. If she did, he might just be angry enough now to deny the friendship, and then later on he'd think he had to stand by the denial. Better to let the dust settle for a minute.

They were finishing the Jell-O when she started again, coming in from another direction entirely, saying, "I read that book again. It isn't bad, you know."

He looked at her. "What book?"

"The one Kelp showed us. The one about the kidnapping."

He straightened and looked around the room, frowning. "I thought I threw that out," he said.

"I got another copy." She'd gotten it from Kelp, but she didn't think she should mention that.

He turned his frown towards her. "What for?"

37

"I wanted to read it again. I wanted to see if maybe Kelp had a good idea after all."

"*Kelp* with a good idea." He finished his Jell-O and reached for his coffee.

"Well, he was smart to bring it around to you," she said. "He wouldn't be able to do it right without you."

"*Kelp* brings a plan to *me*."

"To make it work," she said. "Don't you see? There's a plan there, but you have to convert it to the real world, to the people you've got and the places you'll be and all the rest of it. You'd be the aw-tour."

He cocked his head and studied her. "I'd be the what?"

"I read an article in a magazine," she said. "It was about a theory about movies."

"A theory about movies."

"It's called the aw-tour theory. That's French, it means writer."

He spread his hands. "What the hell have I got to do with the movies?"

"Don't shout at me, John, I'm trying to tell you. The idea is—"

"I'm not shouting," he said. He was getting grumpy.

"All right, you're not shouting. Anyway, the idea is, in movies the writer isn't really the writer. The *real* writer is the director, because he takes what the writer did and he puts it together with the actors and the places where they make the movie and all the things like that."

"The writer isn't the writer," Dortmunder said.

"That's the theory."

"Some theory."

"So they call the director the aw-tour," she explained, "because that's French for writer."

"I don't know what we're talking about," Dortmunder said, "but I think I'm getting caught up in it. Why do they do it in French?"

"I don't know. Maybe because it's more classy. Like chifferobe."

"Like what?"

She could sense the whole thing getting out of hand. "Never mind," she said. "The point was, you could be the aw-tour on this kidnapping idea. Like a movie director."

"Well, I think that whole aw-tour theory is—" He stopped, and his eyes squinted. "Wait a minute," he said. "You want me to do the job!"

She hesitated. She clutched her paper napkin to her bosom. But there was no turning back now. "Yes," she said.

"So you can take care of the kid!"

"Partly," she said. "And also because all of these late-night burglaries aren't good for you, John, they really aren't. You go out and risk life imprisonment for—"

"Don't remind me," he said.

"But I want to remind you. If you get caught again, you're habitual, isn't that right?"

"If I stay away from Kelp," Dortmunder said, "I won't get caught. And if I stay away from him, my luck'll get better. I've had a string of bad luck, and it's all from hanging around with Andy Kelp."

"Like tonight? That store going out of business? You haven't seen Kelp for two weeks, not since you threw him out of here."

"It takes time to wear off a jinx," he said. "Listen, May, I know I'm not pulling my weight around here, but I'll—"

"That's not what I'm talking about, and you know it. These small-time stings just aren't right for you. You need one major job a year, that you can take some time on, do it right, and feel comfortable with a little money in the bank afterwards."

"There aren't any of those jobs any more," he said. "That's the whole problem in a nutshell. Nobody uses cash any more. It's all checks and credit cards. You open a cash register, it's full of nickels and Master Charge receipts. Payrolls are all by check. Do you know, right here in Manhattan, there's a guy sells hot dogs on a street corner, he's on Master Charge?"

May said, "Well, maybe that shows Kelp has a good idea. You can take the story in that book, and adapt it around, and turn it into something. Andy Kelp couldn't do it, John, but you could. And it wouldn't just be following somebody else's plan, you'd *adapt* it, you'd make it *work*. You'd be the aw-tour."

"With Kelp for my actor, huh?"

"I'll tell you the truth, John, I think you're unfair to him. I know he gets too optimistic sometimes, but I really don't think he's a jinx."

"You've seen me work with him," Dortmunder said. "You don't think that's a jinx?"

"You didn't get caught," she pointed out. "You've been collared a few times in your life, John, but it was never while you were working with Andy Kelp."

Dortmunder glowered over that one, but he didn't have an immediate answer. May waited, knowing she'd presented all the arguments she could, and now all she could do was let it percolate through his head.

Dortmunder frowned toward the opposite wall for a while, then grimaced and said, "I don't remember the book so good, I don't know if it was such a hot idea in the first place."

"I've still got it," she said. "You could read it again."

"I didn't like the style," he said.

"It isn't the style, it's the story. Will you read it again?"

He looked at her. She saw he was weakening. "I don't promise anything," he said.

"But you will read it?"

"But I don't promise anything."

Jumping to her feet, she said, "You won't be sorry, John, I know you won't." She kissed him on the forehead, and ran off to the bedroom to where she'd hid the book.

6

KELP WALKED INTO the O. J. Bar and Grill on Amsterdam Avenue at five minutes after ten. He hadn't wanted to make a bad impression by showing up too early, so he'd hung back a little and the result was he was five minutes late.

Two customers at the bar, telephone repairmen with their tool-lined utility belts still on, were discussing the derivation of the word *spic*. "It comes from the word *speak*," one of them was saying. "Like they say all the time, 'I spic English.' So that's why they got the name."

"Naw," the other one said. "It didn't come like that at all. Don't you know? A spic is one of those little knives they use. Din' you ever see one of the women with a spic stuck down inside her stocking?"

The first one said, "Yeah?" He was frowning, apparently trying to see in his mind's eye a spic stuck down inside a woman's stocking.

Kelp walked on down to the far end of the bar. Rollo the bartender, a tall meaty balding blue-jawed fellow in a dirty white shirt and dirty white apron, came moving heavily down the other side of the bar and pushed an empty glass across to him. "The other bourbon's already here," he said. "He's got the bottle."

"Thanks," Kelp said.

Rollo said, "And the draft beer with the salt on the side."

"Right."

"Gonna be any more of you?"

"Naw, just the three of us. See you, Rollo."

"Hey," Rollo said, in a confidential manner, and made a head gesture for Kelp to come in closer.

Kelp went in closer, leaning toward him over the bar. Was there trouble? He said, "Yeah?"

Rollo, in an undertone, said, "They're both crazy," and made another head gesture, this one indicating the two telephone repairmen down at the other end of the bar.

Kelp looked down that way. Crazy? With all those screwdrivers and things, they could get kind of dangerous.

Rollo murmured, "It comes from Spic-and-Span."

A confused vision of people eating a detergent and going crazy entered Kelp's head. Like sniffing airplane glue. He said, "Yeah?"

"On account of the cleaning women," Rollo said.

"Oh," Kelp said. Cleaning women had started it apparently, drinking the stuff. Maybe it was a kind of high. "I'll stick to bourbon," he said and, picked up the empty glass.

"Sure," Rollo said, but as Kelp turned away Rollo began to look confused.

Kelp walked on down past the end of the bar and past the two doors marked with silhouettes of dogs and the words POINTERS and SETTERS, and then on past the phone booth and through the green door at the back and into a small square room with a concrete floor. All the walls of the room were lined floor to ceiling with beer and liquor cases, leaving only enough space in the middle for a battered old table with a green felt top, half a dozen chairs, and a dirty bare bulb with a round green tin reflector hanging low over the table on a long black wire.

Dortmunder and Murch were seated together at the table. A glass was in front of Dortmunder, next to a bottle whose label said AMSTERDAM LIQUOR STORE BOURBON—"OUR OWN BRAND." In front of Murch were a full glass of beer with a fine head on it, and a clear glass saltshaker. Murch was saying to Dortmunder, ". . . through the Midtown Tunnel, and—oh, hi, Kelp."

"Hi. How you doing, Dortmunder?"

"Fine," Dortmunder said. He nodded briefly at Kelp, but then looked away to pick up his glass. Kelp could

42

sense that Dortmunder was still feeling very prickly about this, still wasn't entirely sure he wanted to be friends or go along with this kidnapping idea or anything. May had told Kelp to go slow and easy, not push Dortmunder too hard, and Kelp could see that May had been right.

Murch said, "I was just telling Dortmunder, as long as they've got that construction on the Brooklyn-Queens Expressway, I give up on the Midtown Tunnel at all. At night like this, I can come right up Flatbush, take the Manhattan Bridge, FDR Drive, come through the park at Seventy-ninth Street, and here I am."

"Right," Kelp said. He sat down not too near Dortmunder, and put his glass on the table. "Could I, uh . . ." He gestured at the bottle.

"Help yourself," Dortmunder said. It was brusque, but not really unfriendly.

"Thanks."

While Kelp poured, Murch said, "Of course, going back, what I might try is go down to the *west* side, take the Battery Tunnel, then Atlantic Avenue over to Flatbush, down to Grand Army Plaza, then Eastern Parkway and Rockaway Parkway and I'm home."

"Is that right?" Kelp said.

Dortmunder pulled a paperback book out of his hip pocket and slapped it down on the table. "I read this thing again," he said.

"Oh, yeah?" Kelp sipped at his bourbon.

Dortmunder spread his hands. He shrugged. He seemed to be considering his words very carefully, and finally he said, "It could maybe be used a little."

Kelp found himself grinning, even though he was trying to remain low key. "You really think so?" he said.

"It could maybe be adapted," Dortmunder said. He glanced at Kelp, then looked at the book on the table and gave it a brushing little slap with his fingertips. "We could maybe take some of the ideas," he said, "and work up a plan of our own."

"Well, sure," Kelp said. "That's what I figured." He had his own copy of the book in his jacket pocket. Pulling it out, he said, "The way I saw it—"

"The point is," Dortmunder said, and now he looked directly at Kelp, and even shook a finger, "the point is," he said, "what you got with this book is a springboard. That's all, just a springboard."

"Oh, sure," Kelp said.

"It still needs a *plan*," Dortmunder said.

"Absolutely," Kelp said. "That's why the first thing I thought of, I thought to bring it to you."

Murch said, "What, are we back with that book? I thought we weren't gonna do that."

Dortmunder was being very dignified, very judicious, and Kelp was hanging back and letting him have his head. Turning to Murch now, Dortmunder said, "I give the book another reading. I wanted to be fair, and we don't have that much on the fire that we ought to turn something down without giving it a chance."

"Oh," Murch said. He pulled out a copy of the book and said, "I brought this along to give back to Kelp."

"Well, hold onto it," Kelp told him.

He was immediately sorry, because Dortmunder apparently hadn't liked it. "Hold onto the book if you want," he said, "but what we'll do is, we'll work out our own plan from it. We do what *we* do, not what the book does."

"Sure thing," Kelp said, and tried to flash Murch a high sign that he should go along with it.

Whether Murch saw the sign or not, all he did next was shake his head, look baffled, and say, "Fine with me. You want my Mom in on it?"

"Right. She and May can take care of the kid."

"Okay," Murch said. "Only, where's the kid?"

"Up till now," Dortmunder said, "we're going along with the idea this book can tell us how we get one."

"That's right," Kelp said. "How to find just the kid we want, it's all in the book here."

44

Picking up his copy, Dortmunder said, "Well, I got an open mind. I'm always ready to have a book writer tell me my business. Let's take a look at that part."

Kelp, riffling hurriedly through his own dog-eared copy, said, "It's chapter four. Page twenty-nine."

Dortmunder said, "Thanks," and turned to the right page. He read slowly and patiently, his lips not quite moving, his blunt fingertip following the words from line to line.

Kelp watched him for a few seconds, then began to read the same chapter in his own copy of the book.

Murch sat there by himself. He looked at Dortmunder, and then at Kelp. It took him quite a while to figure out what they were doing; until, in fact, both of them had turned a page. Then he shrugged, picked up his own copy of the book, shook a little salt into his beer to get the head back, drank a bit, and settled down to read.

7

CHAPTER FOUR

When Parker walked into the apartment, Krauss was at the window with the binoculars. He was sitting on a metal folding chair, and his notebook and pen were on another chair next to him. There was no other furniture in the room, which had grey plaster walls from which patterned wallpaper had recently been stripped. Curls of wallpaper lay against the moulding in all the corners. On the floor beside Krauss's chair lay three apple cores.

Krauss turned when Parker shut the door. His eyes looked pale, the skin around them wrinkled, as though he'd spent too long in a swimming pool. He said, "Nothing."

45

Parker crossed the room and looked out the window. A clear blue cloudless day. Three storeys down and one block to the north was the Manhattan exit of the Midtown Tunnel. Two lanes of cars and trucks streamed out of the tunnel, fanning apart into half a dozen lanes of traffic, curving away to the left or the right. Parker watched for a few seconds, then picked up the notebook and studied the entries. The numbers were license plates and dates and times of day. Parker said, "The Pontiac came through today, huh?"

"So did the Mercedes," Krauss said. "But there isn't any phone in either of them."

"We may have to change things around." Parker dropped the notebook on the chair and said, "We'll try the Lincoln today, if it comes through."

Krauss looked at his watch. "Ten, fifteen minutes," he said.

"If it isn't any good," Parker said, "Henley will come take over here at four. If he doesn't show up, that means we're on the Lincoln, so just pack in everything here."

"Right," Krauss said.

Parker glanced out the window again. "See you later," he said, and left the apartment. He went down the warped wooden stairs and out to the street, then crossed Second Avenue and got into a blue Plymouth just around the corner on Thirty-seventh Street.

Henley, at the wheel, said, "Anything new?"

"The Lincoln's still the best bet."

Henley looked in the rearview mirror. "That's due pretty soon, isn't it?"

"Maybe ten minutes."

Henley rolled down his side window and lit one of his narrow cigars. They waited in the car, neither of them saying anything, until Henley, looking in the mirror again, said, "Maybe."

Parker twisted around and looked out the back window. Among the cars crossing Second Avenue, coming this way, was a black Lincoln Continental. Squinting, Parker could make out the uniformed chauffeur at the wheel. "Right," he said.

Henley turned the key in the ignition. When the Lincoln

46

went by, an eight-year-old boy could be seen alone, reading a comic book in the backseat. Henley shifted into drive and eased the Plymouth into line two vehicles back from the Lincoln.

The black car led them across to Park Avenue, then north to Seventy-second Street, then through the park and north again on Central Park West. At Eighty-first Street the Lincoln made a U-turn and stopped in front of the canopied entrance to a large apartment house. Henley eased into a bus-stop zone across the street, and Parker watched as a liveried doorman opened the Lincoln's door, and the boy stepped out, not carrying his comic book. The doorman shut the Lincoln's door and the boy went into the building. The Lincoln moved forward along the kerb and stopped in a no-parking zone just beyond the canopy. The chauffeur took his cap off, picked up a tabloid newspaper from the seat beside him, and settled down to read.

Parker said, "I'll be right back." He got out of the car, crossed the street, and walked slowly down the block past the Lincoln. Looking in on the way by, he saw the telephone built into the back of the front seat. Good. He went on down to the corner, crossed to the park side of the street again, went back to the Plymouth, and slid in next to Henley. "It's got one," he said.

Henley smiled, drawing his lips back to show his teeth clenched on the cigar. "That's nice," he said.

"Now we wait for the kid to come out again," Parker said. "Then we'll take a look at his route home."

8

WHEN DORTMUNDER WALKED into the apartment, Kelp was asleep at the window with the binoculars in his lap. "For Christ's sake," Dortmunder said.

"Huh?" Startled, Kelp sat up, scrabbled for the binoculars, dropped them on the floor, picked them up, slapped them to his face, and stared out at the Lincoln Tunnel exit.

They hadn't been able to find an apartment overlooking the Midtown Tunnel. This one, in a condemned tenement on West Thirty-ninth Street, had an excellent view of the Manhattan exit of the Lincoln Tunnel, bringing cars in from New Jersey. It also, since it faced south, got a terrific amount of sun; even though it was now October, they were all getting sunburns, with white circles around their eyes where they would hold the binoculars.

Kelp was sitting in a maroon armchair with broken springs; this was a furnished apartment, three rooms full of the most awful furniture imaginable. The floor lamps alone were cause for weeping. Kelp's notebook and pen were on a drum table next to him, the drum table having been painted with green enamel and its top having been covered with Contac paper in a floral design. The walls were covered with a patterned wallpaper showing cabbage roses against an endless trellis. Some of this wallpaper had peeled itself off, and curls of it lay against the moulding in all the corners. On the floor beside Kelp's chair stood three empty beer cans and three full beer cans.

Dortmunder slammed the door. "You were asleep," he said.

Kelp put the binoculars down and turned an innocent face. "Huh? I was just resting my eyes a minute."

48

Dortmunder crossed the room and picked up the notebook to study the entries. "You been resting your eyes since one-thirty," he said.

"There wasn't anything useful since one-thirty," Kelp said. "You think chauffeured limousines with a kid alone in the back seat come through every minute?"

"It's all that beer you drink," Dortmunder told him. "You drink that stuff and then you sit in the sun here, and you go to sleep."

"For maybe two minutes," Kelp said. "Maybe at the most five. But not what you could call a *deep* sleep."

Dortmunder shrugged and dropped the notebook back on the drum table. "Anyway," he said, "we've got that Caddy to follow."

"Sure," Kelp said. "It's a natural. And I bet it's got a phone in it. Why else would it have that big antenna thing?"

'Because it's probably the police commissioner of Trenton, New Jersey," Dortmunder said, "and they'll see Murch and me following the car, and we'll get picked up for anarchists."

"Ha ha," Kelp said.

Dortmunder looked out the window. "Traffic," he said.

"You know," Kelp said, "I have a very hopeful feeling about this operation."

"I wish you hadn't told me that," Dortmunder said. He looked at his watch. "If the Caddy's coming through, it'll be pretty soon."

"Sure it's coming through," Kelp said. "Monday, Wednesday, Friday, right around two-thirty."

"Uh huh. If it turns out it's no good, Murch'll come take over here at four. Try to stay awake until then."

"I wasn't really asleep," Kelp said. "Not really. Anyway, I'm wide awake now."

"Uh huh. If Murch doesn't show up here at four, that means we're either following the Caddy or some damn thing has gone wrong, and you should pack up everything and go home."

"Right," Kelp said.

Dortmunder glanced toward the tunnel, looked at Kelp, sighed and said, "See you later."

"Sure."

Dortmunder left and went down the warped wooden stairs and out to the street. He walked to the corner, went a block up Tenth Avenue, and got into the Renault just around the corner on Fortieth Street. Murch, at the wheel, said, "Anything new?"

"Kelp was asleep," Dortmunder said.

"It's all that beer he drinks," Murch said. "He drinks that beer and then he sits in the sun, and he falls asleep."

"I just told him that."

"So what do we do? Follow the Caddy?"

"If it shows up."

"Right." Murch started the Renault, drove a block, waited for a green light, turned left on Dyer Avenue, and parked over against the left-hand kerb.

There wasn't much room in the Renault, and Dortmunder had long legs. While he shifted around, trying to get comfortable, Murch rolled down his side window and took a long narrow cigar out of his shirt pocket. Dortmunder stopped squirming to watch him light it, and then said, "What's that? You don't smoke cigars."

"I thought I'd try one," Murch said.

"It stinks," Dortmunder said.

"You think so? I kind of like it."

Dortmunder shook his head. He scrunched around again, moving himself an inch farther away from Murch, and then rolled his side window down. He hung his right arm outside, and watched the incoming tunnel traffic stream past his right elbow and on up Dyer Avenue.

Dyer Avenue, on the west side of midtown Manhattan, has almost no true existence at all. It runs eight blocks, from Thirty-fourth Street to Forty-second Street, and contains no houses, no shops, no churches or schools or factories. Lined with the blank walls of warehouse backs and overpass supports, it is partially roofed by ramps leading to the upper levels of the Port Authority Bus Terminal, and is used exclusively to funnel traffic coming out of the Lincoln Tunnel. There's no reason to park there, and in fact no parking is permitted.

Which was what the mounted policeman told them, ten minutes later. Coming up on Dortmunder's side of the car, he leaned down beside the neck of his horse and said, "There's no parking here, fella."

Dortmunder looked up and back, and saw this policeman's face suspended in mid-air. Then he saw it was a policeman's head with a horse's body. He just stared.

"Didn't you hear me, fella?" the policeman said.

Dortmunder reared back, as best he could in the Renault, closed one eye, and finally managed to get the right perspective. "Oh," he said. "Right. Yeah." Nodding to the policeman, he turned to tell Murch to drive them away from there.

"Just a minute," the policeman said, and when Dortmunder looked at him again he was climbing down off his horse. *Now what?* Dortmunder thought, and he waited while the policeman got himself down onto the blacktop and leaned his head close to the window. He gave Dortmunder a hard look, and then gave Murch a hard look. He also sniffed loudly, and Dortmunder realized the policeman thought they were drunk. He sniffed again, and wrinkled his face up, and said, "What's that stink?"

"His cigar," Dortmunder said. "I told him it stunk," he said, and watched the Caddy go by. Silver-grey Cadillac limousine, whip antenna, grey-uniformed chauffeur, kid in the backseat, Jersey plate number WAX 361. Dortmunder sighed.

"Urp," Murch said. Then, being very hasty, he said, "Okay, officer, I'll move it now." He even shifted into gear.

51

"Just hold on there," the policeman said. The Cadillac went on up to Forty-second Street and turned right. The policeman, leading his horse, walked slowly in his tight riding boots around the front of the Renault. He studied the car and the license plate, and frowned through the windshield at the two men inside there. Murch gave him a big wide smile, and Dortmunder just looked at him.

There wasn't room for the horse between the left side of the Renault and the brick wall of the overpass support, so the policeman left it standing broadside in front of the car.

Still smiling broadly at the policeman, Murch said out of the corner of his mouth, "What if he asks for license and registration?"

"Maybe there's a registration in the glove compartment."

"Yeah, but I don't have a license."

"Wonderful," Dortmunder said, and the policeman leaned down to look in Murch's window and say, "What are you parked here for, anyway?"

Murch said, "I got a dizzy spell coming through the tunnel." Out front, the horse's tail, which was on Dortmunder's side of the car, lifted up and the horse began to relieve himself.

The policeman said, "Dizzy spell, huh? Let's see you—"

"Your horse," Dortmunder said loudly.

The policeman looked past Murch at Dortmunder. "What?"

"Your horse," Dortmunder said, "is shitting on our car."

The policeman leaned in and looked through the windshield at his horse. "Son of a bitch," he said. He removed his head from the car, went around front, grabbed the reins, and led the horse away from the car.

"Get us out of here," Dortmunder said.

"Right." Murch put the Renault in gear again and angled out away from the kerb and around the policeman and his horse. Moving slowly by, he called to the policeman, "Thank you, officer. I feel a lot better now."

The horse apparently preferred walking to standing still when relieving itself, and was now walking slowly up Dyer Avenue, plopping contentedly behind itself, and ignoring the policeman's efforts to make it stop. "Yeah yeah," the policeman said, nodding in distraction at Murch, and to the horse said, "Stop there, Abner, stop there."

Up at Forty-second Street the light was against them. They stopped, and Dortmunder said, "Goddam it to hell and goddam it back again."

"So we'll try it again Friday," Murch said.

"The horse'll shit in the window next time."

The light turned green and Murch made a left. "You want me to take you home?"

"Might as well."

At Tenth Avenue the light was against them. Murch said, "I threw out the cigar, did you notice?"

"I told you it stunk."

"Friday we'll wait around the corner on Forty-second. You can park there."

"Sure," Dortmunder said.

The light remained red. Murch looked thoughtful. He said, "Listen, you in a hurry?"

"In a hurry for what?"

"Let's take a little drive, okay?"

Dortmunder shrugged. "Do what you want."

"Fine," Murch said. The light turned green and he headed up Tenth Avenue.

Dortmunder brooded for forty blocks, as Tenth Avenue changed its name to Amsterdam Avenue and its language to Spanish, but as they crossed Eighty-sixth Street he finally sat up, looked out at the world, and said, "Where we going?"

"Up to Ninety-sixth," Murch said, "and over to Central Park West, and then down. After that I'll take you home."

"What's the idea?"

53

Murch shrugged, and seemed slightly embarrassed. "Well, you never know," he said.

"You never know what?"

"In the book, the car goes to Central Park West."

Dortmunder stared at him. "You think the Caddy's going to be on Central Park West because the car in the *book* was on Central Park West?"

Murch showing increasing discomfort. "I figured," he said, "what the hell, it won't cost us anything. Besides, in the book the kid's coming in for special speech therapy, right? So this kid, in the Caddy, he's got to be coming in to see some specialist like that, too, and Central Park West is full of those guys."

"So's Park Avenue," Dortmunder said. "So's a lot of other places, all over town."

"If you don't want to do it," Murch said, "it's okay with me. I just figured, what the hell."

Dortmunder looked at the sign for the cross street they were passing: Ninety-fourth. "You want to go to Ninety-sixth, and then down?"

"Right."

"Well, we're here already, so go ahead."

"It probably won't come out to anything," Murch said, "but the way I figured, what—"

"Yeah, I know," Dortmunder said. 'You figured, what the hell."

"That's the way I figured," Murch said, and made the turn on Ninety-sixth Street. They travelled two blocks to Central Park West, turned right again, and headed south, with the park on their left and the tall apartment buildings on their right. They travelled south for twenty-five blocks, Murch looking more and more awkward and Dortmunder feeling more and more fatalistic, when all of a sudden Murch slammed on the brakes and shouted, "Son of a *bitch!*"

A cab behind them honked, squealed its brakes, and twisted on around them with various words shouted out into the air. Dortmunder looked where Murch was pointing, and he said, "I just don't believe it."

The Caddy. Silver-grey, whip antenna, Jersey plate number WAX 361. Parked in a bus stop, big as life. When Murch drove slowly by, the chauffeur was sitting behind the wheel in there reading a tabloid newspaper. His hat was off.

Murch found a space in front of a fire hydrant in the next block. He was grinning all over his face when he switched the engine off and turned to say to Dortmunder, "I just had a hunch, that's all. I figured, what the hell, and I just had a hunch."

"Yeah," Dortmunder said.

"You get things like that sometimes," Murch said. "It's just a hunch you get, they come on you sometimes."

Dortmunder nodded, heavily. "We'll pay for this later on," he said, and got out of the car, and walked back up toward the Cadillac. It was parked facing this way, and the chauffeur's head was hidden behind his open newspaper.

Dortmunder didn't look right on Central Park West, and he knew it. He felt eyes on him, mistrusting him. It seemed to him that doormen, as he walked by, glared at him and clutched their whistles. Cruising cabs accelerated. Dog walkers stood closer to their Weimaraners and Schnauzers. And old men in wheelchairs, being pushed by stout black ladies in white uniforms, scrabbled at their blankets.

Dortmunder walked slowly by the Cadillac. The back seat was empty and the side windows were open, but it was very hard to see inside. Aware of being an alien here, still feeling the eyes on him, Dortmunder didn't want to stop, so he kept on walking even though he didn't know if there was a telephone in the limousine or not.

Well, he couldn't keep walking north forever. At the next corner he stopped, looked indecisive, then patted himself all over, pantomiming a search for some small but necessary object. In a large elaborate movement, he snapped his fingers, suggesting the sudden realization that the small but necessary object had been left behind; at home, perhaps. He then turned around and walked the other way.

The Cadillac was getting closer. Coming from behind it he had a clearer view of the interior, but it still wasn't good enough. He walked more and more slowly, squinting, trying to see into the damn car.

Well, screw it. He went over to the Cadillac, leaned down, stuck his head in the open window by the back seat, and saw that indeed there was a telephone mounted on the back of the front seat. He nodded in satisfaction. The chauffeur remained inside his newspaper.

Dortmunder got his head out of the Cadillac and walked briskly on down to the Renault. He opened the Renault door, but before getting in he looked back up at the Cadillac. The chauffeur still hadn't moved, but as Dortmunder watched he suddenly jumped, yanked the newspaper down into his lap, spun around and stared at the empty back seat. He then faced front again, looking baffled. He turned his head this way and that, staring suspiciously all around. His eyes met Dortmunder's, and he frowned, deeply.

Dortmunder got into the Renault. He arranged his feet as best he could, closed the door, and said, "The amazing thing is, there's a goddam telephone in there."

Murch was still grinning from ear to ear, and he had his paperback copy of *Child Heist* open in his hands. "Now we wait for the kid to come out again," he said, reading the words from the book. "Then we'll take a look at his route home." He slapped the book shut and said, "Just like it says in the book!"

"Yeah," said Dortmunder.

9

WHEN DORTMUNDER ESCORTED May into the O. J. Bar and Grill, Rollo the bartender was in the process of separating two customers who had come to blows during a statistical discussion of the New York Mets. Stools and chairs were being kicked as the customers thrashed around on the floor with their arms around one another. Rollo, avoiding their feet, circled them looking for an opening. Dortmunder gestured for May to move off to the left, and the two of them got in behind the cigarette machine, in the front corner of the room.

"So this is the O. J.," May said, as a stool went crashing over on its side. The seat part of the stool separated from the chrome legs and went rolling away toward the rear, making metal noises on the floor. The three other customers in the place were all straining toward the television set, trying to make out what George Peppard was saying to Jill St. John.

"It's usually quieter than this," Dortmunder said.

Out there on the floor, Rollo had gotten hold of a shoulder and was shaking it. Then, with his other hand, he got hold of a different shoulder and tried throwing it away. The shoulders, though wearing different colored jackets, didn't want to separate at first; Rollo had to do a lot of shaking with his left hand while making three strong throwing gestures with his right before they popped apart. Then the one customer went skidding away on his back under a booth, and Rollo picked the other one up by his shoulder and hair and carried him to the front door. On his way by the cigarette machine he nodded to Dortmunder and said, "How ya doin?"

"Fine," Dortmunder said.

Rollo pushed the door open with the customer's head, and ejected the customer. Then he turned and went back for the other customer, who was scrambling out from under the booth. Rollo picked him up by his belt, in the middle of his back, and half-carried half-ran him across the floor and through the door and out onto Amsterdam Avenue. When he came back in, he nodded again to Dortmunder, who was escorting May out from behind the cigarette machine, and said, "When he asked for white cream de mint I knew there was gonna be trouble."

"Rollo," Dortmunder said, "this is May."

"How ya doin?" Rollo said.

"I'm fine," said May. "Does that happen a lot?"

"Not so much," Rollo said. "We mostly got beer drinkers in here. Beer drinkers got a low center of gravity, they don't like to fight much. They just like to sit there, mind their own business."

"I like a nice beer myself," May said.

"I seen you were a good person when you walked in," Rollo said. To Dortmunder he said, "The other bourbon's in the back. I give him your glass."

"Okay."

"Expecting anybody else?"

"The draft beer and salt," Dortmunder said. "And he'll be bringing his mother."

"Oh, yeah, I remember her. She's also a draft beer, right?"

"Right."

"That's nice," Rollo said. "I like ladies in the place, it makes for a better atmosphere."

"Thank you," May said.

"You go on back," Rollo said, "I'll bring you your beer, little lady."

Dortmunder and May went to the back room, and Kelp was sitting there with the bottle of bourbon and two glasses.

He got to his feet and said, "Hi, May. Sit down. What was all the noise out there?"

"That was Rollo," Dortmunder said, "cutting back on his services."

"He's very gallant," May said.

Kelp, looking at his watch, said, "Murch and his Mom are late."

Dortmunder nodded. "I know. And the worst of it is, he'll tell us why."

"And," Kelp said, "what route he should of took."

May said, "Maybe he couldn't find a deserted farmhouse."

Kelp said, "Why not? We found the kid, didn't we? We followed the book and we found the kid. So now the book says we want a deserted farmhouse, we'll find a deserted farmhouse."

Dortmunder said, "You know, there are these little moments when that book gives me a swift pain in the ass."

"It's been right so far," Kelp said. "You got to give credit where credit is due."

May said, "Tell me about this boy. John says you found out about his family and all."

"Right," Kelp said. "His name is Jimmy Harrington. His father's a lawyer on Wall Street, in the firm of McIntire, Loeb, Sanderson and Chen. He's a partner there."

Dortmunder said, "He's a partner? I thought his name was Harrington."

"It is," Kelp said.

"There isn't any Harrington in the company name. Just those other people."

"McIntire," Kelp said, "Loeb, Sanderson and Chen."

"Right," Dortmunder said. "That bunch. If Harrington's a partner, where's his name?"

"They got a whole bunch of partners," Kelp said. "I saw a piece of their stationery, there's this whole line of names down the left side, they're *all* partners. I think maybe McIntire, Loeb, Sanderson and Chen are maybe the *first* partners."

"The founders," May suggested.

"I get it," Dortmunder said. "Okay, fine."

"Anyway," Kelp said, "Harrington is maybe fifty-five, he's got four grown-up kids and grandchildren, the whole thing. He's also got a second wife, and she's got grown-up kids. But when they got married they had a kid together, and that's Jimmy. The father's name is Herbert and the mother's name is Claire."

"I feel sorry for the mother," May said. "She's going to feel terrible."

"Maybe," Kelp said. "She and Herbert broke up six years ago, she lives down in Palm Beach, Florida. From what I found out so far, she hasn't been north in six years, and I don't think Jimmy travels south. Jimmy lives out on the family estate in New Jersey, way over by Pennsylvania."

Rollo came in with May's beer while Kelp was saying that; he put it on the table, looked around, and said, "Everybody set?"

"We're fine," Dortmunder said.

"The beer and salt and his mother didn't show up yet," Rollo said.

"They'll be along," Dortmunder said.

"I'll send them back," Rollo said, and went out front again.

May said to Kelp, "How did you find out all this?"

"There's a little town out near the estate," Kelp said. "I went out there and hung around in a bar and talked to a couple guys. The guy that drives the oil truck that makes deliveries there, and a carpenter that did some work on the estate, and a bulldozer operator that worked there when they put in their swimming pool a couple years ago."

"They didn't have a swimming pool before?" May asked.

"No. The estate's on the Delaware River. Only I guess

the river isn't so hot for swimming any more. Anyway, these guys told me the story. Workmen like to talk about their rich clients, it's one of their fringe benefits."

"Sure," May said. "So the mother left six years ago, and the boy lives on the estate with his father."

"Sometimes," Kelp said. "The father has an apartment in town. The kid comes in three afternoons a week, Monday and Wednesday and Friday, and sees some specialist in that apartment building on Central Park West. Fridays, after he's done there—"

"What specialist does he see?"

"I can't find out," Kelp said. "There's all kinds of medical people, and specialty therapists, and I don't know what in that building. And it's tough to hang around in there. And the maintenance people don't know Jimmy Harrington from a special delivery letter. Anyway, when he leaves there on Fridays, he goes down to Wall Street in the limousine, and his father rides out to the estate with him. The father stays there all weekend, and rides in with him on Mondays. But Monday to Friday the father stays in town."

"The boy's all *alone* out in the estate?" May was truly shocked.

"There's four servants that live in," Kelp said. "The chauffeur, and the—"

The door opened and Murch's Mom came in, followed by Murch. They were both carrying beers, and Murch was also carrying a saltshaker. May looked up and said, "So *there* you are."

"It's real nice out there," Murch's Mom said. She sat down at the table, placing the beer in front of her. "Especially at this time of year, with the leaves all turning."

"We thought you got lost," May said.

"Naw," Murch said. "It's simple. You go out 80, you get off at the Hope interchange, you take county road 519. Our big problem was, we had a hell of a time finding an abandoned farmhouse."

"I knew it," Dortmunder said. He gave a triumphant

61

glare toward the book lying on the table in front of Kelp.

Kelp said, "But you did find one, huh?"

"Yeah, finally." Murch shook his head. "All the abandoned farmhouses out there, people from the city already went out and found them and bought them and filled them up with fancy barn siding and cloth wallpaper and made country houses out of them."

"They've all got Great Danes," Murch's Mom said. "We went out some of those driveways pretty fast."

"But the point is," Kelp said, "you did find an abandoned farmhouse."

"It's a mess," Murch said. "There isn't any electricity, and there isn't any plumbing. There's a well out back, with a handle thing that you pump."

Murch's Mom nodded. "It's not like anything in the twentieth century," she said.

"But it's isolated," Kelp suggested. "Is it?"

"Oh, yeah," Murch said. "It's isolated, all right. Way to hell and gone isolated."

"Well, that's the important part," Kelp said. Primarily speaking to Dortmunder, he said, "We'll only be there for a couple days, and the more abandoned and isolated it is the better."

Dortmunder said to Murch, "How far is this from where we grab the kid?"

"Maybe twenty miles."

"And how far from the kid's house?"

"Maybe forty."

Dortmunder nodded thoughtfully. "It's kind of close," he said.

Kelp said, "That's got a big advantage, when you think about it. The cops won't be looking in that close."

"The cops," Dortmunder told him, "will be looking *everywhere*. A rich man's son is gone, they'll look for him."

"If they find that abandoned farmhouse," Murch said, "I'll be surprised."

"We'll all be surprised," Dortmunder said. "Unpleasantly."

"I'll tell you something else," Murch said. "Last night I started reading again the chapter where they do the kidnapping. You know, where they go and grab the kid."

"Chapter eight," Kelp said. "Page seventy-three."

Dortmunder gave him a look. "You memorized it?"

"I'm just careful, that's all," Kelp said.

"Anyway," Murch said, "we got a hell of a lot of stuff we're supposed to put together for that job. Not just the abandoned farmhouse and the side road and all that, but a lot of *stuff*, you know."

"Not that much," Kelp said. "Just a couple things."

"Not that much?" Murch started counting them off on his fingers. "A big tractor-trailer rig. A school bus. A car. Guns. Mickey Mouse masks. A detour sign."

"None of that is tough," Kelp said. "I can get the car myself, I'll borrow one from a doctor."

"The tractor-trailer? The school bus?"

"We'll pick them up," Kelp said. "Don't worry about it, Stan, we can do it. The detour sign I'll paint myself and bring it along."

"It's a lot of stuff," Murch said.

"Just don't worry about it," Kelp told him.

May said, "Let's get back to the boy. How old is he?"

"Twelve," Kelp told her. "That's the adventurous age, May. The kid'll have a ball, it'll be like living out one of his favorite television shows."

"I'm beginning to feel sorry for him anyway," May said, "even if we *don't* take him. Living all alone with nobody around but servants, hasn't seen his mother since he was six years old. That's no life for a little boy."

Kelp said, "So this'll make a nice change."

May stared at him. "To kidnap him? A nice change?"

"Why not?" Kelp seemed perfectly sincere about it. "A break in the routine, everybody likes that."

"I just wish I knew," May said, "what kind of specialist

63

he goes to when he comes to the city."

"Maybe it's a speech therapist," Kelp suggested, "like the kid in the book."

Dortmunder plunked his glass down on the table. Exasperated, he said, "How many coincidences you want out of that book?"

"Well, what difference does it make anyway?" Kelp shrugged. "The point is, he comes to the city on a regular schedule."

May said, "I was just thinking about special medicines or treatments or something that we might have to have."

"He looks healthy, May," Kelp said. "Besides, we'll only have him a day or two. He probably won't even miss a session."

"I'd still like to know who he sees," May said. "Just what kind of specialist. Just to know."

10

JIMMY HARRINGTON, LYING on the black naugahyde couch in Dr. Schraubenzieher's office, looking over at the pumpkin-colored drapes half-closed over the air-shaft window, said, "You know, for the last few weeks, every time I come into the city I keep having this feeling, *someone is watching me.*"

"Mm hm?"

"A very specific kind of watching," Jimmy said, "I have this feeling, *I'm somebody's target.* Like a sniper's target. Like the man in the tower in Austin, Texas."

"Mm hm?"

"That's obviously paranoid, of course," Jimmy said. "And yet it doesn't truly have a paranoid *feel* about it. I think I understand paranoid manifestations, and this seems somehow to be something else. Do you have any ideas, Doctor?"

"Well," Dr. Schraubenzieher said, "why don't we study the implications? You feel that you are being watched, that you are somehow a target. Is that right?"

"That's right. A very specific sensation of eyes, of being observed for some *purpose*. It's like that well-known phenomenon of being on a plane and feeling that one is under observation, and then looking around to see that some other passenger actually is looking at you."

"And in the current situation? Is anyone actually looking at you?"

Jimmy frowned at the drapes. They moved slightly, stirred by the quiet air-conditioner in the wall below. "I don't know," he said. "So far I haven't caught anyone at it."

"*Caught* anyone? A very suggestive phrase, that."

"But that's the way it feels." Jimmy concentrated, trying to get in touch with his feelings. He'd been in analysis for nearly four years, and was very professional about it by now. "There's an element of . . . sport in it," he said. "As though it's a game, and I win if I catch them looking at me. I know that sounds childish, but that is the sensation."

"As I am forced to remind you frequently, Jimmy," Dr. Schraubenzieher said mildly, "you *are* a child. A childlike response, even from you, is not necessarily a negative event."

"I know," Jimmy said. One of his unresolved and so-far unstated disagreements with the doctor concerned this aspect of childlike behavior; Jimmy felt that his own disapproval of such behavior in himself was so instinctive and so strong that it simply had to be trusted. He was not, however, prepared as yet to debate the issue with Dr. Schraubenzieher, so he altered the subject slightly, saying, "Why did you say that 'caught anyone' was a suggestive phrase?"

"You know very well why," the doctor said; he himself knew very well why Jimmy was veering away from the topic of childishness, but he wouldn't push the matter. In the course of the analysis the debate must eventually arise, and it would be better to wait for Jimmy to feel strong enough to raise the subject himself.

At the moment, Jimmy had hared off after this semantic scent. "I don't see that 'caught anyone' is a particularly pertinent phrase," he said. "It's merely the standard idiom in that circumstance, normal American usage: 'I caught him looking at me' is simply the way that's *said*. I suppose it's the mind's instinctive aversion to the duplication of idea implicit in 'I *saw* him *looking*.' On the other hand, I could merely be evading the issue, analysing it away."

"One of the great problems in analysis," the doctor said, "is that the patient may merely become cleverer at avoiding self-comprehension. To evade my suggestion by offering the titillation of a friendly discussion on idiomatic usage is wily enough, but then to suggest *yourself* that you are trying an evasion technique is almost too clever. The idea being, of course, that we will now go off on the tangent of your evasion mechanisms, and therefore safely avoid discussion of either your dislike of childhood mannerisms or your fear of competition."

"Fear of competition?" Once again Jimmy avoided the childish-behavior problem, this time realizing just a second too late that in dodging away from that he had landed himself squarely in the topic the doctor *really* wanted to discuss. Before seeing the trap, though, he had already blundered ahead by asking, "Where does that come in? We weren't discussing my fear of competition."

"Oh, but we were," the doctor said, and Jimmy could hear the smugness of victory in the man's voice. "You spoke of being someone's target. You said it was like a sport or a game. You said you hadn't caught anyone yet, but that you felt if you did catch someone you would win."

"I think you're just playing semantics with me."

"You mean you'd rather I would play semantics with you. But I won't. I will instead point out that in being in the top two percentile of IQ, you naturally know that you stand out from your peers, even among the boys of Bradley School. Being wealthy also sets you apart. You are inevitably and naturally the target of many eyes. You have been taught that much is expected of you, and you are aware of the level of performance that you *should* be capable of maintaining. Your competition is with your own excellence, it is played out very much in public, and you fear your inadequacy to maintain your own standard. Thus your desire to make motion pictures, to be the director and have the opportunity to safely be in charge; first to define the action and then to capture it permanently on film, where it can't get out of your control."

"I thought we'd agreed," Jimmy said coldly, "not to mention that ambition of mine."

"You're right," the doctor said. "I do apologize."

The fact was, the only time Jimmy had ever demonstrated real anger toward Dr. Schraubenzieher had been on this subject of movies. He knew that he wanted to make movies because he was an artist; the doctor, assuming him to be a child, assumed the desire to be childish. He had asked for movie equipment, and the Christmas before last he had been given a Super 8 silent camera and projector. Super 8! Would they have given Mozart a toy piano? Wasn't Mozart a child?

Well, he'd been through those arguments, to no effect. Except that this last Christmas he'd been given some basic 16-mm equipment, with a potential capacity for sound. Still, it wasn't home movies he was interested in, it was film art.

But they weren't going to talk about that; it had been agreed, after his one outburst, to let the subject lie. The doctor had made a mistake in bringing it up, but had immediately apologized, and that at least was something. Jimmy, who had gone rigid, relaxed again and said, "I'm sorry. Where were we? Competition with myself, wasn't it?"

"Exactly. Competition with your own high standard.

67

Thus your fear of being childlike, as though to act your age would be somehow to fail to live up to your potential. You have a brilliant mind—for your age. You are extremely imaginative and resourceful—for your age."

"But isn't there a fallacy," Jimmy asked, "in the concept of competition with one's own capabilities? There can't be failure, because an apparent failure would merely indicate a faulty original estimate of the capabilities. The estimate should then be geared down to the actual accomplishment, thus obliterating the apparent failure. And if failure is impossible, ipso facto victory is also impossible. Without the potential for either victory or failure, how can there be competition?"

Dr. Schraubenzieher smiled at the back of the boy's head. Very well, he would give the child a rest; particularly since Jimmy had behaved so decently about the motion picture slip. For the remainder of the session they played word games.

At the end, when Jimmy was leaving the consulting room, he paused in the doorway, looked at the doctor with a troubled frown, and said, "Do you suppose by any chance somebody *is* watching me?"

The doctor smiled indulgently. *He's projecting the motion picture director theme,* he thought, but of course didn't say that. "Certainly not," he said. "We both know better, don't we?"

"I suppose so. See you Friday."

11

KELP, SITTING IN the back seat with the Mickey Mouse masks, said, "Here he comes."

"I see him," Dortmunder said. Dortmunder was driving, and May was sitting next to him. Kelp was the one who had gotten this car, a blue Caprice with MD plates, and it had been his intention to drive it, but Dortmunder had said, "I'll drive." No explanation, just a sort of heavy determination that Kelp had found it impossible to argue with. So Kelp was now in the back seat, leaning forward between Dortmunder and May, watching through the windshield as the kid—somewhat tall for his age, but very skinny—came out of the apartment building and was escorted into the grey Cadillac by the doorman.

Dortmunder started the engine of the Caprice. Kelp said, "You don't want to follow too close. Hang back a couple cars."

"Shut up, Andy," Dortmunder said, and May turned to look at Kelp and give him a little nod, suggesting that he should humor Dortmunder at the moment by leaving him alone.

"Anything you say," Kelp said, and relaxed against the seat back as Dortmunder eased the Caprice into the line of traffic.

The Cadillac led the way down Central Park West to Sixty-ninth Street, then across to Ninth Avenue and straight down to the Lincoln Tunnel. It was shortly after four on a Wednesday afternoon, and the rush-hour traffic had already started to build. It was stop-and-go through the tunnel, but over on the Jersey side things loosened up, and they were driving almost up to the speed limit as they headed west, across route 3.

Kelp had been nervous and full of anticipation all day, but now that they were actually in motion he found himself growing increasingly calm. In fact, sitting in the back seat of a car heading west across New Jersey was essentially a dull and monotonous occupation no matter what the purpose, and Kelp soon had to admit he was getting bored. Conversation might have helped, but he suspected Dortmunder wasn't in any mood for chitchat, and in any event it's always hard to maintain a conversation between the front and back seats of an automobile. So after a while he pulled from his pocket one of his copies of *Child Heist* and began to read again the part where they grabbed the kid. Chapter eight.

12

CHAPTER EIGHT

When Parker got to the intersection he made a U-turn and stopped, facing back the way he had come. He and Angie waited in the Dodge while Henley took the ROAD CLOSED— DETOUR sign out of the trunk and set it up blocking the numbered county road, with the arrow pointing toward the smaller blacktop road leading off into the woods to the right. This was a completely empty intersection, the crossing of a minor county road and an almost-abandoned old connector road, with no buildings of any kind anywhere in sight. On two sides there were dense woods, on the third a scruffy weed-grown meadow, and on the fourth a cornfield now dry and brown after the harvest.

Henley got back into the car, and Parker drove a quarter mile back toward the city, then backed off into the dead-end dirt road he'd found last week. There was nothing to do now but wait; Krauss and Ruth had already been dropped off, Krauss would be setting up the other detour sign, and everything was set.

Six miles away, the black Lincoln limousine took the curving ramp down from Northern State Parkway to the county road and turned north. The chauffeur, Albert Judson, drove steadily at fifty-five, undisturbed by other traffic in this sparsely populated area early on a Tuesday afternoon. In the back seat, Bobby Myers read his comic books, sprawling comfortably across the seat.

Seven minutes later Henley said, "Here they come."

70

"I see them," Parker said, and put the Dodge in gear as the Lincoln sailed by them. The Dodge moved out from the dirt road and accelerated in the Lincoln's wake.

Judson, at the wheel of the Lincoln, tapped the brake when he saw the sign blocking the road ahead. Bobby, behind him, looked up from his comic book and said, "What's the matter?"

"Detour. We have to take Edgehill Road."

"The detour wasn't there before."

Judson, turning off onto the secondary road, said, "I guess they just started. Maybe they'll fill in those potholes down by the bridge."

"Boy, I hope so," Bobby said. "Sometimes I could throw up along there."

"Don't do that," Judson said, grinning in the rear-view mirror at the boy, and as he did so he came around a curve in the road and saw vehicles stopped ahead. A school bus, facing this way, its red lights flashing, meaning it was unloading passengers and traffic wasn't permitted to pass it in either direction. And a truck, a big tractor-trailer rig, facing the same direction as the Lincoln and obediently standing still. The two vehicles between them blocked the road completely. Judson braked, and the Lincoln slid to a stop directly behind the truck.

Bobby said, "Why's the bus stopped there?"

"Must be letting somebody off."

"Nobody's getting out."

Judson, who was sometimes irritated by Bobby's questions, said, "Then they're waiting for somebody who's supposed to get on."

Back at the intersection, Parker stopped long enough for Henley to get out and move the detour sign so that it now blocked the road the Lincoln had just gone down. Then they drove on, following the Lincoln.

Judson too was beginning to think the school bus was taking too long to do nothing. Glancing in the rear-view mirror again, seeing the blue Dodge coming to a stop behind him, almost close enough to touch the Lincoln's rear bumper, he said, "Pretty well-travelled road."

In the Dodge, Parker and Henley and Angie were putting on the large rubber Mickey Mouse masks. "I feel like a clown in this thing," Henley said. His voice was muffled and altered by the rubber.

"It's to make it easier for the kid," Parker said. "We don't want a hysterical kid on our hands. Angie, you do the talking to him."

"Right."

"It's a game, it's fun, we're all just playing."

"I know," Angie said.

"Let's go," Parker said.

They got out of the Dodge, Parker and Henley carrying revolvers, and walked swiftly up next to the Lincoln, Parker on the left and Henley and Angie on the right.

Judson, who was frowning now toward the school bus, wondering why it wasn't finishing its business and moving on, caught a glimpse of something moving in his outside mirror. He looked at it, and saw a man coming this way with something glittery and strange over his head. "What the—?" He twisted around to his left, to look back, and the man closed the distance, pulled open Judson's door, and said, fast and low, "Not a move. Not one move."

There was a gun in the man's hand, down by Judson's elbow. "Uh," said Judson. The Lincoln's engine was running, but the gearshift was in park. Also, the car was wedged in both front and back by the truck and the Dodge. Still, Judson's hand started to move almost instinctively toward the gearshift lever, when the door on the passenger side opened, and another one got in. Another gun, another mask over the head. Judson, looking at him, suddenly terrified at this apparition sitting next to him, realized what he was looking at was a Mickey Mouse mask, and for some reason that only made things more frightening.

Meanwhile, Angie had gotten into the backseat. "Hi,

Bobby," she said. "Do you know whose face this is I'm wearing?"

Bobby hadn't seen the guns of the two men dealing with the chauffeur, but he'd heard the toughness in the one man's voice, and he sensed the strangeness of what was happening. Frightened, not sure what to expect or how he should act, he said, "Who—who are you?"

"Who do I look like, Bobby?"

"You're not Mickey Mouse!" He knew that much; and being able to say so, loud and clear, helped to calm and reassure him.

"But I'm making believe to be Mickey Mouse," Angie said. "We're all going to play make-believe for a while now."

Up front, Henley had pressed his revolver into Albert Judson's side. His voice soft, muffled by the mask, he said, "Let's not scare the kid. Nobody's gonna get hurt."

"What do you—?" Judson's mouth was dry. He coughed, and started again. "What do you want?"

"Think about it," Henley said.

Parker, seeing that the chauffeur was under control, shut the Lincoln's door again and went up to rap on the rear doors of the tractor-trailer. The doors swung open, pushed out by Krauss, who looked critically out and down at the Lincoln and said, "You'll have to back it up."

"I know."

Parker walked back past the Lincoln to the Dodge. Inside the Lincoln, Henley was controlling the chauffeur and Angie was controlling the boy. She was talking to him, chattering at him, keeping him calm with a soothing flow of words.

Parker got into the Dodge, ran it backward about fifteen feet, got out of it, walked up to the Lincoln, opened the chauffeur's door again, and said, "Slide over."

Henley made room, and Judson slid over into the middle of the seat. He said, "You're going to kidnap the boy!"

Henley said, "Keep it down. I told you, we don't scare the kid."

Krauss had pulled the metal ramp out of the truck partway

and now, when Parker put the Lincoln into reverse and backed up till he was nudging the Dodge's bumper, Krauss brought the ramp out of the rest of the way and lowered it to the ground. Parker shifted into low and eased the Lincoln forward, up the ramp and inside the truck.

Bobby, wide-eyed, said. "What are we doing?"

"Have you ever been inside a truck before?" Angie tried to make it sound like a treat, or a game. "Inside a *car* that's inside a truck?"

"I don't think I want to do this," Bobby said.

"Don't be afraid, Bobby," Angie said. "Nobody's going to hurt you, I promise."

Parker switched off the Lincoln's engine, took the keys, and climbed out. It was a tight fit between the side of the car and the inner wall of the truck. Parker went sideways to the rear of the truck, dropped down to the ground, and helped Krauss slide the ramp back up inside the truck.

In the Lincoln, Judson had moved over behind the wheel again; not so he could drive, but so he would be farther from the gun. Henley, facing him but staying on his own said, said, "Switch on the interior lights," and Judson did so, without question.

Parker and Krauss closed the truck's doors; inside, now, the only illumination came from the lights inside the Lincoln. Bobby, his fright being slowly overcome by curiosity as time went by with no attack against him, looked around and said, "It's like being out at night, isn't it?"

"That's right," Angie said. "We'll pretend we're going for a drive now, at night."

Outside, Krauss and Parker had removed their masks. Ruth, at the wheel of the school bus, switched off the flashing red lights, put the bus in gear, and drove it off the road. Krauss got into the cab of the truck, started the engine, and drove off, accelerating slowly, the engine whining up through the gears.

Ruth got out of the bus and walked across the road to the Dodge. Peeling rubber gloves from her hands, she tossed them into the weeds beside the road, then got into the Dodge on the passenger side as Parker slid in behind the wheel. She said, "How'd the kid take it?"

"Fine," Parker said. "Angie's talking to him."

Parker swung the Dodge around in a U-turn, drove back to the intersection, and picked up the detour sign there. He tossed it in the trunk, went back the other way again, passed the abandoned school bus, and caught up with the tractor-trailer at the next crossroad, where Krauss was removing the second detour sign, the one that had diverted traffic away from Edgehill Road while they were collecting the Lincoln.

Inside the Lincoln, Henley had taken out the handcuffs, and cuffed the chauffeur to the steering wheel. Now, when Krauss knocked on the trailer doors, Henley turned to Angie, nodded at the boy, and said, "Get him ready."

"I know." Despite the muffling effect of the mask, Angie's nervousness could clearly be heard, and she fumbled at first when she tried to take the other mask out from under her shirt. Then she got it, and showed it to Bobby, and said, "This is for you. The same kind of mask as the rest of us, see? Mickey Mouse."

"For me?" Then he looked at it more closely, and said, "The eyes are taped up."

"That's because we're going to go on playing night-time," Angie said. "We'll be leaving the truck now, but you're still going to make believe it's night."

"I won't be able to see anything!" Renewed fright made the boy's voice shrill.

"You'll be holding my hand," Angie told him. "It's all right, it really is. Ask your chauffeur, there, he knows."

Bobby looked doubtfully toward Judson, whose back was to him. "Albert?" he said. "Am I supposed to do that?"

Judson turned his head just enough to see Henley and the gun in Henley's hand. "Answer the boy," Henley said, his voice soft. He was holding the gun too low for the boy to see it.

Judson nodded. Not facing Bobby, he said, "It's all right, Bobby. You do what these people say. There's nothing to worry about."

75

Bobby relaxed a bit, then, but still kept looking doubtfully at everybody, and when he said, "All right, then, I'll wear the old mask," his reluctance was clear in his voice.

Angie slipped the mask on over the boy's head. "Is that all right? It isn't too tight, is it?"

"No, it's okay. It smells funny." His voice, too, was muffled now.

"That's the smell of rubber," Angie told him. "Take my hand, now, we're going to get out of the car."

Henley led the way, opening the rear doors of the truck, then handing Bobby down to Parker. Angie got down, took the boy's hand again, and led him over to the Dodge. Henley and Krauss closed the truck doors while Parker got into the Dodge and started the engine. Angie and Henley had gotten rid of their masks now, leaving Bobby the only one with his face covered.

They all got into the Dodge, the three men in front, the two women in back with the boy between them. Angie said, "Bobby, this is Gloria, a friend of mine."

"Hello, Bobby."

Bobby said, his face toward Angie, "You took your mask off. Your voice sounds different."

"You're the one with the mask on now," Angie told him. "We take turns."

"And be sure to leave it on," Ruth said. She sounded colder, more stern than Angie.

"I will," Bobby said. Angie had been continuing to hold his hand, and now Bobby squeezed her fingers, holding on.

13

WHEN DORTMUNDER GOT to the intersection he made a U-turn and stopped, facing back the way he had come. He and May waited in the Caprice while Kelp got out and went around to the back of the car. Then he came around to the side again, rapped on Dortmunder's window, and when Dortmunder rolled the window down Kelp said, "I need the key."

"The what?"

"The key. For the trunk."

"Oh." The keys were all together on a key ring. Dortmunder switched off the engine and gave the keys to Kelp, who went and unlocked the trunk, then gave the keys to Dortmunder, then went back and got his sign. He stood there holding it, looking around but not doing anything, until Dortmunder leaned his head out and yelled, "What are you doing?"

"I forgot which one to block."

Dortmunder pointed. "That one. The one on the kid's route."

"Oh, yeah. Right."

Kelp went over and set up the sign. It was a three-by-four piece of thin metal that had once advertised 7-Up, and the shape of the bottle could still be seen vaguely through the yellow paint. Kelp had also thought to bring a triangular arrangement of sticks to lean the sign against, a detail not mentioned in *Child Heist*. He put the sign in place, then trotted back over to the Caprice and said, "How's that?"

Dortmunder looked at it. It said ROAD CLOSED—DETURE. He said, "Jesus H. Goddam Christ."

"What's the matter?" Kelp looked all around the intersection, worried. "Did I put it in the wrong place?"

"Do you have that goddam book on you?"

"Sure," Kelp said.

"Take it out," Dortmunder said, "and find the page where they set up the sign." Turning to May, he said, "I'm following a book he read, and he doesn't even know *how* to read."

Kelp said, "I got it."

"Look at it. Now look at the sign."

Kelp looked at the book. He looked at the sign. He

77

said, "Son of a gun. Detour. I thought *sure* you—"

"You can't even *read*! "

May said, "It's okay, John, it really is. They'll just think some local highway department people didn't know how to spell."

Dortmunder considered that. "You think so?"

Kelp hopped into the back seat. "Sure," he said. "It makes it more realistic, like. Who'd expect a kidnap gang to put up a sign that's spelled wrong?"

"I would," Dortmunder said. "In fact, I'm surprised I didn't think to check."

"Listen, I don't want to push you," Kelp said, "but we ought to get down there to that dirt road."

"I wonder what next," Dortmunder said. He started the engine, drove a quarter mile back toward the city, then backed off into the dead-end dirt road Murch had been astonished to find last week.

"Now there's nothing to do but wait," Kelp said.

"I'll lay five to two," Dortmunder said, "some farmer comes along in a pickup truck, drives in, wants to know what we're doing here, and pulls out a shotgun."

"You're on," Kelp said.

Four miles away, the silver-grey Cadillac limousine took the curving ramp down from Interstate 80 to the county road and turned south. The chauffeur, Maurice K. Van Gelden, drove at varying speeds above fifty-five, competing with the occasional other car he met. In the back-seat, Jimmy Harrington read the "Letter from Washington" in the current *New Yorker* and wished he had the self-confidence to tell Maurice to quit racing the other drivers. Maurice behaved himself when Jimmy's father was in the car, but when it was just Jimmy back there he obviously thought he could get away with being a cowboy. And the annoying part of it was, he could; Jimmy wouldn't complain to his father, since that would be the act of a baby, but on the other hand he hadn't yet felt quite secure enough to complain to Maurice directly.

Pretty soon I will, Jimmy thought, and read about the administration's hopes for a settlement in the Middle East.

Five minutes later, May and Kelp both simultaneously said, "Here they come."

"I see them," Dortmunder said, and put the Caprice in gear as the Cadillac rocketed by them. The Caprice moved out from the dirt road and accelerated in the Cadillac's wake.

"That's five dollars you owe me," Kelp said.

Dortmunder didn't answer.

Van Gelden, at the wheel of the Cadillac, suddenly slammed on the brakes and swerved all over the road when he saw the sign blocking the road ahead. Jimmy, flung off the seat, came sputtering up, crying, "Maurice! What in the name of God is going on?"

"Goddam deture!" Van Gelden cried. He thought the word was spelled that way.

Jimmy got one quick flashing glimpse of the sign as the Cadillac slewed around, tyres squealing, and reared off down the secondary road. "Detour?" He frowned out the back window; there's been something about that sign, he wasn't sure what. It had gone by so fast. As a soft drink commercial's jingle started up in his brain, distracting him, he said to himself, "The detour wasn't there before."

This secondary road was narrower, bumpier, and curvier than the county road. Van Gelden, taking out his rage at the fact of the deture by flinging the car forward as rapidly as possible, was tossing Jimmy around the back seat like a sneaker in a dryer. Jimmy, holding on for dear life, found at last the maturity to shout out, "Damn it, Maurice, *slow down!*"

Van Gelden didn't touch the brake, but he did lift his foot from the accelerator. "I'm just trying to get you home," he snarled, glaring in the rearview mirror at the boy, and as he did so he came around a curve in the road and saw vehicles stopped ahead. A school bus, facing this way, its red lights flashing, meaning it was unloading passengers and traffic wasn't permitted to pass it in either direction. And a truck, a big tractor-trailer rig, facing the same direction as the Cadillac and obediently standing still. The two vehicles between them blocked the road completely.

"Goddamit," Van Gelden said, and tromped on the brake again. He had to brake hard to stop in time, but it was less violent than if his foot had still been pressed on the accelerator when he'd rounded the bend. Jimmy, since he'd been clutching the armrest and a strap anyway, managed to stay on the seat as the Cadillac nosed down to a shuddering stop directly behind the tractor-trailer.

"One thing after another," Van Gelden said.

"Maurice," Jimmy said, "you drive too fast."

"It's not my fault there's all this stuff in the way." Van Gelden gestured angrily toward the truck and the bus.

"You drive too fast all the time," Jimmy insisted. "Except when my father is in the car. From now on, I want you to drive me the way you drive my father."

Van Gelden, becoming sullen, jammed his uniform cap farther down on his forehead, folded his arms, and said nothing.

Jimmy said, "Did you hear me, Maurice?"

"I hear you."

"What?"

"*I hear you!*"

"Thank you, Maurice," Jimmy said, and sat back to savor his triumph. After a moment he picked up the *New Yorker* again.

Back at the intersection, Dortmunder stopped the Caprice and Kelp jumped out to move the sign. He picked it up, moved it to another side, and started back, when Dortmunder leaned out the window and shouted, "Not there! Where we follow the Cadillac! "

"Huh?" Kelp looked around, pointing at various places, reorienting himself. Then, with a sudden sunny smile of recognition, he waved to Dortmunder and shouted, "Gotcha!" He ran back to the sign, picked it up, and put it back where it had been.

"Not *there*!" Dortmunder yelled. He was leaning his whole upper torso out of the car, pounding the door panel with his arm and the flat of his hand. Waving that hand violently around, he yelled. "Over *there*!"

"Right!" Kelp yelled. "Right! Right. I got it now!" And he picked up the sign and started trotting toward the last possible wrong choice.

Dortmunder came boiling out of the Caprice. "I'm going to wrap that sign around your *head*!"

"*Now* what?" Kelp stood there, bewildered, while Dortmunder came over and wrenched the sign and sticks away from him and put them where they belonged. Kelp watched, and when Dortmunder was finished the two men met again at the car, where Kelp said, "I would have got it, I really would have."

"Get in the car," Dortmunder said. He got behind the wheel and slammed the door.

Kelp got in the back seat again. May shook her head at him, not pleased, and he lifted his shoulders helplessly. Dortmunder punched the accelerator, and the Caprice bounced forward.

Van Gelden, his sullenness boiling over all at once into rage, pushed the button that rolled his window down, stuck his head out, and yelled toward the school bus, "Get with it, will ya! We don't have all day!"

Jimmy looked up from his magazine. "What's the matter, Maurice?"

"Bus just *sitting* there," Van Gelden said. "Tying up traffic." Looking in the rearview mirror, he said, "And here comes somebody else."

Jimmy looked back, and saw the blue car approaching around the curve. The road here was hemmed in by trees and shrubbery on both sides. Scrub pine gave some swaths of green, but the rest of the trees had lost about half their foliage, making black trunks and branches form jagged

81

lines against the orange and gold of autumn leaves. Dead leaves swirled around the tyres of the blue car as it came silently toward them, slowed, and stopped. The figures through the windshield were indistinct, but in some sort of motion back there.

Jimmy faced front again. The woods were close on both sides, the rear of the tractor-trailer was like a looming silver wall directly in front of the Cadillac, and leaves kept fluttering down off the trees, rustling down past the windows. The driver of the school bus was a vague mound through the big flat windshield; afternoon sunlight glinted from that windshield, reddish-yellow with a bright white center.

"There's something wrong," Jimmy said.

"What?" Van Gelden looked at Jimmy in the rearview mirror, and caught a glimpse of somebody going by with a Mickey Mouse mask on his head. "What the hell?"

Jimmy said, "What?" and his right-hand door opened, and a woman wearing a Mickey Mouse mask slid in. "Hi, Jimmy," she said. Her voice was so muffled by the mask he could barely make out what she was saying. It was, "Do you know whose face this is I'm wearing?"

Dortmunder, trotting forward, yanked at the driver's door, but it was locked. Van Gelden, seeing the big man with the jacket and the Mickey Mouse mask and the gun, pushed the button again to roll his window back up, but Dortmunder stuck the barrel through the diminishing space and said, "Stop that. Stop it now."

Van Gelden released the button. He blinked at the gun barrel pointing more or less at him.

Jimmy, not only knowing whose face the woman was wearing but also realizing at once why she was wearing it, reached out for the telephone. May, expecting a dialogue on the subject of Mickey Mouse, was too startled to react until the boy had already dialled Operator. Then she grabbed for the phone, saying, "Stop that! Don't be like that!"

82

Kelp, reaching the passenger door on the front right, found it locked and looked across the top of the Cadillac at Dortmunder. "Make him unlock it," he said.

Dortmunder said, "Unlock the doors. Make it snappy."

A switch on the driver's door would lock or unlock all the others. Van Gelden, also realizing right away what these people had to be up to, and seeing no point in making trouble for himself in a situation where he was essentially an innocent bystander, pushed the switch and unlocked the doors. He also slid his window open again.

In the back seat, May had finally wrestled the telephone out of Jimmy's hands and disconnected the bewildered operator. "Now," she said, panting from exertion, "we're going to play make-believe. I'm going to make believe I'm Mickey Mouse, and you're going to make believe you can behave."

"Kidnapping," Jimmy said, "is a Federal offense. Conviction carries a mandatory life sentence."

"Just be quiet," May said. "I'm here to soothe you, and you're making me upset."

In the front seat, Kelp had entered and was holding a gun pointed at the chauffeur. Every time he inhaled, the rubber mask pressed itself to his face. He was getting enough air, but nevertheless he felt as though he was suffocating. His voice garbled by the mask, he said, "Let's not scare the kid. Nobody's gonna get hurt."

Van Gelden said, "What? I don't know what you're saying."

Holding the mask out from his mouth with his free hand, Kelp said, "Let's not scare the kid. Nobody's gonna get hurt." It was a line word for word from *Child Heist*, which Kelp had been rehearsing for two weeks now.

According to the book, the chauffeur was now supposed to ask Kelp what he wanted. Instead of which, Van Gelden pointed at the pistol and said, "Scare the *kid*?" Then he gestured a thumb over his shoulder and said, "Scare *that* kid? Hah!"

83

Kelp's memorized response didn't suit any of that, so he stayed silent.

Dortmunder, meantime, had gone around to the rear doors of the tractor-trailer. He rapped on them, and the doors swung open, pushed out by Murch, also in a Mickey Mouse mask. He looked critically out and down at the Cadillac and said, "You'll have to back it up. Just like in the book."

"I know," Dortmunder said. Just like in the book. Dortmunder turned and walked back past the Cadillac toward the Caprice. Inside the Cadillac, Kelp's Mickey Mouse face was staring at the chauffeur and May's Mickey Mouse face was staring at the boy. She was supposed to be chattering at him, keeping him calm with a soothing flow of words, but she was just staring at him. They seemed to have some sort of Mexican standoff in there.

Dortmunder backed up the Caprice, then walked to the Cadillac again, opened the chauffeur's door and said, "Move over."

Kelp made room, and Van Gelden slid over into the middle of the seat. He said, "I hope you birds are bright enough to surrender if some state trooper happens by. I don't want to be a hostage or a victim or anything like that."

Kelp, given an opportunity to produce another of his lines from the book, said, "Keep it down. I told you, we don't scare the kid."

But he'd said it without lifting his mask away from his mouth. Van Gelden looked at him and said, "What?"

"Forget it," Kelp said.

"What?"

Kelp took the mask away from his mouth. "Forget it! "

"You don't have to shout, fella," Van Gelden said. "I'm right next to you."

Dortmunder started the Cadillac and backed it away from the truck. Then Murch pulled out the two wooden planks they were going to use instead of a metal ramp. May

84

was the one who had pointed out that if they used a ramp they wouldn't be able to put it back in after the car was inside the truck, since the car's wheels would be in the way. Dortmunder had said, "And that's the book we're supposed to follow," but Murch had immediately suggested a pair of planks, which could be stored under the Cadillac once it was inside.

But it took a while to place them. Dortmunder sat with both hands on the wheel, and Murch kept running back and forth between the truck and the car, making minor shifts in the two planks, lining them up with the front wheels and trying to keep them nice and parallel. Finally, content, he climbed up into the truck and gestured for Dortmunder to drive forward.

Slowly they went up the ramp. They could feel the planks bending beneath the weight, but Murch had positioned them properly and the tyres were nicely in the middle of each plank. The front tyres; the rear tyres were still on the ground when the bumper scraped against the rear of the truck.

"Now what?" Dortmunder said.

Murch, frowning, went to look at the left front fender of the Cadillac, and then at the right front fender. He shook his head, frowned more deeply, put his hands on his hips, and went back to consider the left front fender again. Then, leaning on that fender, he called to Dortmunder, "It's too wide! "

Dortmunder stuck his head out the side window. "What do you mean it's too wide?"

"It won't fit."

Murch backed up from the Cadillac, standing inside the truck and studying the two vehicles. He held his hands up, palms facing one another, and peered through them. He shook his head.

Murch's Mom, sitting at the wheel of the school bus and not knowing what the *hell* was going on, considered honking the horn to try to attract somebody's attention.

But probably this wasn't a good time to distract them all from whatever they were doing over there. On the other hand, it did seem to be taking them a long time to get that Cadillac into that truck.

Inside the Cadillac, Kelp said, "I never heard of such a thing. Cars always fit inside trucks."

Van Gelden said, "What?"

"Nothing," Kelp said.

"I should have known," Dortmunder said.

Jimmy, in the back seat, found himself considering the situation as though it were a problem to be solved. Like the problems in *Scientific American*, to which he was a subscriber. But that wasn't the right thing to do; he wasn't on their side, he was on the other side. So he tabled the problem, to be considered at some later time.

May, leaning forward, said, "Maybe we could—" and the phone rang.

Everybody jumped. The Cadillac sagged on the boards. May stared at the phone in horror and said, "What do I do?"

Dortmunder twisted around. It was hard, with three men crammed in together in the front seat, but he turned sufficiently to be able to look through the eyeholes in his Mickey Mouse mask at both May and the boy. He said, "The kid has to answer it."

The phone rang again.

Dortmunder said to the boy, "You play it like everything's okay. You got the idea?"

"I won't cause any trouble," Jimmy said. He wasn't exactly frightened of these people, but he was well aware that a tense situation could sometimes make a person react more violently than they would normally. He didn't want any of this gang going into a panic.

"You just answer the phone," Dortmunder said. "You act normal, and you make it as short as you can."

"All right," Jimmy said. He reached out to pick up the phone as it rang for the third time.

Dortmunder said, "Hold it away from your ear, so we can all hear what they're saying."

Jimmy nodded. His mouth and throat were dry. Picking up the phone, he held it so the back part was out and away from his ear. "Hello?"

"Hel-lo, there, is this James Harrington?" The cheerful male voice came tinnily from the phone.

"Yes, it is."

"Well, this is Bob Dodge of radio WRTZ, the voice of Sussex County, calling you from Hotline For Facts. Your postcard has been selected at random, and you have the opportunity to win prizes totalling over *five hundred dollars*! And now, here's Lou Sweet to tell you what prizes are in this week's Hotline Jackpot!"

Another voice began to ripple from the phone, describing prizes, in each case giving the name of the merchant who had contributed the prize. A camera from a drugstore. Dog food from a supermarket. A dictionary and a table radio from a department store. Dinner for two at a local restaurant.

"I don't believe this," Dortmunder said, and May shushed him again.

Bob Dodge came back on the phone. "Are you familiar with the rules of our game?" he asked, but before Jimmy could answer he gave them anyway, talking at top speed. There seemed to be something about levels, options of subject matter, various other sophistications, but the main idea was that they would ask him questions and he would try to answer them. "Are you ready, James?"

"Yes, sir," Jimmy said. He sometimes listened to this program in the car on the way home from Dr. Schraubenzieher, and it always seemed as though he knew the right answers whenever the contestants got them wrong. About six months ago he'd sent in a postcard, giving both his home phone and the mobile telephone unit in the car, but he'd never expected them to call him. Particularly not the mobile telephone number.

87

And he sure wished it hadn't happened now. It was embarrassing to be here on the phone like this, answering some quiz show's silly questions, with a lot of strangers looking on.

"And here's your first question," Bob Dodge said. "Name four of the states of Australia."

Australia. Concentrating. Jimmy said, "New South Wales, Queensland, Victoria. And Northern Territory."

"Very good! Next, give the atomic number of samarium."

"Sixty-two."

"What is hemialgia?"

"Pain on one side of the head."

"I've got pain on both sides of my head," Dortmunder muttered.

"Sshh!" Kelp said.

"Who wrote *Adrienne Toner*?"

"Anne Sedgwick."

'What year was the battle of Lancaster Abbey?"

Jimmy hesitated. The others in the car all tensed, looking at him, waiting. Finally, with the question apparent in his voice, he said, "Fourteen ninety-three?"

"Yes!"

Everybody in the car sighed with relief; three Mickey Mouse masks ballooned.

Jimmy answered four more questions, on astronomy, economics, French history and physics, and then the next question was, "In astrology, what are the signs before and after Gemini?"

Astrology; that was one of Jimmy's weak areas. He had no belief in it, and so had never studied it. He said, "The signs before and after?"

"Before and after Gemini, yes."

"Before Gemini . . . is Taurus."

"Yes! And after?"

"After Gemini."

Kelp whispered, "Cancer."

Dortmunder glared at him. He whispered, "If you're wrong—"

"Time is almost up, James."

Jimmy took a deep breath. He didn't like accepting help on a test, but what else could he do? He hadn't asked for it, and it might not even be right. He said, "Cancer?"

"*Absolutely right!*"

Again, general relief. Even with the mask over his face, Kelp could be seen smiling.

"You, James Harrington," Bob Dodge was saying, "have won our Hotline Jackpot!"

"Thank you," Jimmy said, and when he saw Dortmunder gesturing violently at him he added, "I have to hang up now," and hung up.

"Well," May said. "Jimmy, that was really impressive."

"Okay," Dortmunder said. 'Now that the kid got his dog food and his dinner for two, let's get back to—"

And the planks gave way; both of them at once. The Cadillac slapped down onto the road like a palm slapping down on a table. Everybody was tossed up, ricocheted off the roof, and jolted into their seats again. In the process, Dortmunder's gun went sailing out the open window next to him, and Kelp's gun bounced off the roof, the steering wheel and the dashboard before landing in Van Gelden's lap.

"Hands up!" Van Gelden yelled, and scrabbled in his lap for the gun. Both Dortmunder and Kelp were obediently lifting their arms, and Van Gelden was still bobbling the gun, when May reached over his shoulder, took it away from him, and handed it to Dortmunder.

"All right," Dortmunder said. "All right, that's enough fooling around." To May he said, "Put the mask on the kid and put him in our car." To Kelp he said, "Put the cuffs on this guy. If it won't upset you too much, we're gonna rewrite that book of yours a little bit."

"Anything you say," Kelp said. He was pulling the handcuffs out of his hip pocket.

"And you," Dortmunder told the chauffeur, "you just sit there and keep your mouth shut. 'Hands up,' is it?" Giving the chauffeur a look of disgust that the chauffeur couldn't see through the Mickey Mouse mask, Dortmunder got out of the Cadillac, picked up his gun from the road, and said to Murch, "Forget that goddamn truck. We'll go straight to the hideout from here. All that other crap was more complicated than it had to be anyway."

"Right," Murch said. "I'll get my Mom," he said, and jumped down out of the truck.

May had put the Mickey Mouse mask with the taped eyeholes over Jimmy's head. She'd considered using the dialogue from the book about pretending it was night and all that, but somehow it didn't seem to fit the case, so all she'd said was, "I'm going to blindfold you now."

"Of course," Jimmy said.

Murch rid himself of his mask and went over to the school bus, where his Mom was impatiently tapping her fingernails on the steering wheel. She pushed the lever on her left, the door accordioned open, and she said, "So? You want to tell me something?"

"We're all taking off in our car, Mom. Run the bus out of the way and come on over."

"I been sitting here," she said. "Wondering what's going on."

"It would take a while to tell, Mom."

"I saw the Caddy bounce," she said.

"That was part of it."

"I wish I had springs like that in the cab," she said. "Climb aboard." She shifted into first, and Murch stepped up into the bus as she eased it forward and off onto the shoulder of the road.

May had now led the boy from the Cadillac to the back seat of the Caprice, Kelp had handcuffed Van Gelden to the steering wheel, and Dortmunder had filled his pockets with guns and was standing beside the Cadillac looking mulish. When Murch and his Mom came over from the school bus Dortmunder said, "Stan, you drive."

"Right."

Murch's Mom got in the back seat with May and Jimmy. "Well, hello, Jimmy," she said. "I see you're playing Mickey Mouse."

May shook her head. "It's not quite like that," she said.

Inside his mask, Jimmy said, "I really am a bit old for this kind of psychological reassurance."

"Hmp," Murch's Mom said. "A smart alec."

In the front seat, Kelp sat in the middle, with Murch on his left and Dortmunder on his right. As Murch started the engine, Kelp said to Dortmunder, "Can I have my gun back?"

"No," Dortmunder said. He looked around at the setting they were leaving, giving everything the same impartial look of disgust: truck, school bus, planks, Cadillac, chauffeur. "Hands up," he muttered, and the Caprice drove off in a flurry of falling leaves.

14

DORTMUNDER SAID, "WHAT'S taking so long? We been driving for forty-five minutes."

"I've been taking some extra turns and cutbacks," Murch said, "to confuse the boy's sense of direction. That's what they did in the book."

"In the meantime," Dortmunder said, "the cops are out looking by now."

"We should have picked up the detour signs," Kelp said. "We shouldn't have left them behind like that."

"We don't need them any more," Dortmunder told him. "And I don't want to waste any more time." To Murch he said, "So let's go straight to the farmhouse. No more extra turns."

"Well," Murch said.

Dortmunder looked at him. "What do you mean, well?"

"Well, the fact is," Murch said. He was blinking a lot as he drove, and looking troubled, even embarrassed. "The fact is," he said, "I think I took too many extra turns and cutbacks already."

"You're *lost*?"

"Well," Murch said, "not exactly lost."

"What do you mean, not *exactly* lost?"

"Well, there was a road I thought was down this way, and it isn't here. I can't seem to find it."

"If you can't seem to find the road you're looking for," Dortmunder said, "that means you're lost. *Exactly* lost."

"It would help if the sun was out," Murch said. It was late afternoon now, and the sky was filling with clouds.

"I think it's gonna rain," Kelp said.

Dortmunder nodded. "And we're lost."

"If I take the next left," Murch said, "we should be all right."

"You think so," Dortmunder said.

"Maybe," Murch said.

15

"THERE IT IS," Murch said. "This time I'm positive."

"The last time you were positive," Kelp said, "I almost got bit by a dog."

The three men peered squinting out of the windshield, through the streaming sheets of rain at the structure vaguely showing in the headlights. This was the fourth dirt road they'd taken since the simultaneous arrival of darkness and rain, and tempers in the car were generally frayed. Jimmy had gone to sleep, with his head propped against May's arm, but everybody else was wide awake and jittery. Twice on other dirt roads they'd become stuck in the mud, and Kelp and Dortmunder had had to get out and push. Once, when they'd found a house that had looked right to Murch, they'd discovered just after Kelp got out of the car that it was the wrong house, occupied by several human beings and at least one big German shepherd.

"Right house or wrong house," Dortmunder said, "just don't get us stuck again."

"I'm doing my best," Murch said. "Besides, that's definitely the right house."

"I'm your mother, Stan," Murch's Mom said, "and I'll tell you right now, if you're wrong again, don't ever stand in front of my cab."

Murch, leaning forward over the steering wheel, scrinching his face up as he tried to see, kept the gearshift in low and his foot gently on the accelerator. They thumped and jounced slowly through the potholes, and the structure out front gradually became more and more visible. A house, weathered clapboard, with an open front porch. Boarded-up windows. No lights anywhere.

"It *is* the right house!" Murch cried. "By golly, it really *is!*"

"How come you sound surprised?" Dortmunder asked him, but Murch's Mom was leaning forward, her head between Dortmunder and her son, and she said, "Stan, you're right. That's the place, it definitely is."

"By golly," Murch said. "By golly."

The dirt road made a sweep around the front of the house, then petered away into the woods to the right. Murch jounced them as close to the stoop as he could, then stopped the car and said, "We made it."

"Leave the headlights on," Dortmunder told him.

In the back seat, the stopping of the car had awakened

Jimmy. Sitting up, trying to rub his eyes and discovering he had some sort of rubber thing over his head, he said, "Hey!"

"Take it easy, Jimmy," May said, patting him soothingly on the arm. "Everything's all right."

In darkness, his head covered by something that both felt and smelled unpleasant, surrounded by strangers whose voices he didn't recognize, Jimmy felt a swift moment of panic. Reality and dream swam together in his mind, and he had no idea where he was or what was happening or what was real.

But after a person has been in analysis for nearly four years, it becomes second nature to automatically study and dissect all dreams and dream fragments. With his mind busily seeking the symbolic content of darkness, rubber masks, and strange voices, he couldn't completely lose control, or remain panic-stricken for very long. "Oh," he said, sighing with relief, "it's just the kidnappers."

"That's right," May said. "Nothing to worry about."

"I was really scared for a second there," he said.

"We're going to get out of the car now," May told him. "It's raining, and we have some stairs to go up, so hold my hand."

"All right."

They transferred themselves from car to house, getting drenched in the process, and Murch, coming last, switched off the headlights before going up into the house.

It had apparently been several years since anybody had lived here. Except for a nonworking gas stove in the kitchen, a framed newspaper photograph of moon-walking astronauts on the wall in the living room, and a badly stained mattress in one of the bedrooms upstairs, the place had been completely empty when Murch and his Mom had found it. Since then, they'd driven out three carloads of furnishings, and Murch had discovered that the toilet upstairs would work if the tank was filled with buckets full of water from the hand-pump well in the back yard. "The only thing is," he'd told the others earlier, "you don't flush for everything."

May and Murch's Mom led Jimmy directly upstairs, lighting their way with two of the flashlights Murch had brought out on one of his earlier trips. The bedroom they'd chosen didn't have bars over the windows, like the room in *Child Heist*, but it did have boards nailed over the windows, which was just as good. And it had a solid door that could be locked with a key from the outside.

May had carried her mask up with her, and Murch's Mom had borrowed her son's; they put them both on now, before taking Jimmy's mask off. May said, "This is where you're going to live for the next day or two. Until we get the money from your father."

Jimmy looked around. Vaguely in the beams of the two flashlights he could see the cot with pyjamas laid out on it, and the folding chair piled with half a dozen comic books. The two windows were both covered with boards on the outside. "It's cold in here," he said.

"There's lots of blankets on the bed," May told him. "And I'll bring you up some hot dinner pretty soon."

The two women started to leave, and Jimmy said, "May I keep one of the flashlights? So I can read the comic books."

"Sure," May said, and gave him hers. Then she and Murch's Mom went out to the hall and took their masks off again. They locked the door, left the key in the lock, and went downstairs.

Murch had lit the three kerosene lanterns he'd stashed here, and the living room looked almost liveable. Wet clothing now hung from the nails and hooks left in the walls. Kelp was sitting at the card table in his undershirt, playing solitaire, and Dortmunder was wringing out his shirt. The smell of wet cloth mixed with the odor of kerosene smoke; combined with the boarded-up windows and the exaggerated shadows on the walls and the darkness beyond the

95

interior doorways, it was more like being in a cave underground than in a house.

Dortmunder said, "The kid okay?"

Murch's Mom said, "He's in better shape than we are."

"I'll get us something to eat," May said, and went over to the stone fireplace in the corner of the room. Murch had brought out charcoal and a hibachi, two large cans to boil water in, and some field rations nicknamed Lurps; officially Long Range Reconnaissance Patrol Rations, they were dry rations in plastic bags, which converted into casseroles like beef-and-rice or pork-and-beans when hot water was added. There were also instant coffee, Pream, and plastic cups and dishes.

Dortmunder said to Murch, "You drive your mother to a phone booth now. You can find one, can't you?"

Murch was astonished. "Go out *now*? In that rain?"

May, her hands full of Lurps, said, "You've got to let the boy's father know he's all right."

"Sure," Dortmunder said. "There's also the little matter of the ransom." To Murch's Mom he said, "You know what to say?"

"Why not?" She patted her jacket pocket. "I'll just read it to him out of the book."

"The book," Dortmunder said sourly. "Yeah, that's fine."

"And when you come back," May said, "I'll have some nice warm dinner for you."

"Hah!" shouted Kelp, and slapped a card down on the table with such force that everybody jumped and stared at him. "I got it out!" he said, and gave everybody a happy smile. At their frowning expressions, he exclaimed, "That doesn't happen very much."

"It better not," Dortmunder said.

16

USING THE FLASHLIGHT sparingly, Jimmy pulled out the center double-page from one of the comic books, smoothed the crease in its middle by running it back and forth over the edge of the folding chair's seat, and then slid it carefully under the hall door, directly beneath the knob. They hadn't bothered to search him, so he still had his ballpoint pen, the inner cartridge of which was both thin enough and rigid enough to fit into the keyhole and slowly push the key out the other side.

Plink.

After that tiny sound, of the key hitting the comic book sheet on the hall floor, Jimmy waited, tense, his ear to the keyhole, until he was sure the sound had not been heard downstairs. Then, slowly, carefully, he drew the sheet of paper back into the room, and there was the key, athwart Jughead.

Operating now in darkness, the flashlight in his hip pocket, Jimmy unlocked the door and tiptoed out to the corridor. Could it really be this easy, or were they testing his resourcefulness, leaving one of them hidden on guard upstairs here, to see what he might do?

But apparently not. A little light showed from his right, and when he moved that way he could hear the voices downstairs. He already knew there were five of them, and when he reached the head of the stairs and looked down all five were there. One of the men and the older woman were putting on coats. The other woman was fiddling with a hibachi in the fireplace. The second man was playing solitaire at a card table (and from the looks of things cheating), and the third one was prowling back and forth, holding a wet shirt out and shaking it as though to hurry its drying.

Five. They were either underestimating him or over-estimating themselves; probably both. He waited till the couple with coats on went out and then, turning away from the staircase, he went exploring.

It took ten minutes to discover that all the windows up here were boarded, and that there was no second staircase down. He also discovered, in that time, a wire coat-hanger, an eight-inch-piece of galvanized pipe, and a half-full squirt can of 3-in-1 oil.

But the big finds were in the attic, which he gained access to via a trapdoor in a bedroom closet. In the mountain school in Switzerland last summer he'd learned the chimney climb, going up funnel-type openings by pressing one's back against one side and walking one's feet up the other. He went up the closet walls that way, got into the attic, and made both finds almost at once. In an old metal toolbox were several rusty abandoned tools: a hammer, a screwdriver, pliers, a long slender tweezers. And off in a corner, behind several stacks of *Grit*, was a good long coil of rope.

Pleased with himself, Jimmy used the rope to lower the toolbox, then dropped the rest of the rope down after it and walked his way back down the closet walls. It took two trips to carry everything back to his room, and on the second trip he paused at the head of the stairs again to see how his kidnappers were doing. The woman was now boiling water on the hibachi, and the two men were playing rummy. From the looks of things the woman would be bringing him food pretty soon so he shouldn't stand around here wasting time.

Going back to his room, he put the key in the lock on the outside, went into the room, and pulled the door shut. Then, using the tweezers from the toolbox, he carefully turned the key from inside; one revolution all the way around and the lock clicked into place.

Now, to work.

17

HANGING UP THE phone after talking with the kidnapper, Herbert Harrington said, "Well. I can't say I cared for *that* at all."

"Let's listen to it," the head FBI man said, and they all waited in silence while the technician ran the tape back to the beginning again.

Herbert Harrington plucked his white handkerchief from his suit coat's breast pocket and patted the tiny beads of perspiration that gleamed on his pale high forehead. A calm, methodical, successful corporation attorney of fifty-seven, he was used to emergencies and crises that ran at a Wall Street pace: weeks of gathering storm clouds, spotted with occasional conferences or public rumor denials, then a flurry of phone calls, a massing of capital along the disputed border, and then perhaps three days or a week or even a month of concentrated buying, selling, merging, bankruptcy declarations and the like. Drama with sweep to it, emotional climaxes as carefully grounded and prepared for as in grand opera.

But *this*. They kidnap the boy at four o'clock in the afternoon, and by nine o'clock the same night they're demanding one hundred fifty thousand dollars for him. In old bills. In an equivalent situation on Wall Street, it would be three or four working days before anybody even admitted the boy had been taken. *Then*, there'd be a period of weeks or months when the kidnappers would publicly maintain the posture that they meant to keep the boy, had no interest in selling him, and wouldn't even consider any offers that might come their way. This logjam, assisted by continued denials from Herbert Harrington or his spokesmen that (a) he was interested in negotiating a repurchase, (b) that he was in a cash or tax position to make such a repurchase possible, or (c) that in fact he had ever had such a son at all, would eventually be broken by tentative feelers from both sides. Bickering, threats, go-betweens, all the panoply of negotiation would then be mounted and gone through like the ritual of High Mass, and it would be even more weeks before anything like a dollar amount was ever *mentioned*. And in fact dollars would be the very least of it; there would be stock options, rebates, one-for-one stock transfers, sliding scales, an agreement with some *meat* on it. Instead of which—

"All set," the tape technician said.

"Run it," the head FBI man said. They all talked in clipped little sentences like that; Harrington felt himself getting a headache.

From the machine, a voice said, "Hello?" and another voice said, "Is that Herbert Har—"

Talking over the second voice, Harrington said, "Is that me? It doesn't sound like me."

"Hold it," the head FBI man said, and the technician stopped the tape and ran it backward again. To Harrington the head FBI man said, "Let's just listen."

"Oh, of course," Harrington said. "I'm sorry, I didn't mean to interrupt, I was merely startled."

"Run it," the head FBI man said, and the tape started forward again.

"Hello?" His own voice sounded lighter to him than he would have guessed; not so manly. He didn't much like it.

"Is that Herbert Harrington?" It was a female voice, middle-aged, New York City accent, rather truculent. An irascible-sounding woman, like one of your lady cab-drivers.

"Yes, it is. Who's calling, please?"

"We have your boy."

"I beg your pardon?"

"I said, 'We have your boy.' It means we kidnapped

him, we're the kidnappers. I'm one of the kidnappers, this is the phone call."

"Oh, yes! Of course, I'm sorry. Maurice phoned me when he got home."

"What?"

"My chauffeur. He was very upset, he said it was extremely difficult to drive while chained to the steering wheel."

Small pause. Then, the woman's voice again: "Look, let's start all over. We have your boy."

"Yes, you said that. And this is the phone call."

"Right. All right. Your Bobby's fine. And he'll—"

"What say?"

"I said, 'Your Bobby's fine. And he'll stay—"

"Are you sure you have the right number?"

"Jimmy! I didn't mean—I meant Jimmy. Your *Jimmy's* fine. And he'll stay fine just as long as you cooperate."

Silence. Far in the background one of those telephone company noises took place: boop-boop-boop-boop-boop-boop-*beep*-boop-boop-boop.

The woman's voice: "Did you hear me?"

"Yes, of course."

"Well? You gonna cooperate or aren't you gonna cooperate?"

"Of course I'll cooperate."

"At last. Okay. That's good. And the first thing is, you don't call the police."

"Oh, dear."

"What?"

"I do wish you'd told me before. Or told Maurice, that would have been best."

"What the hell are you talking about?"

"Well, the fact is, I've already called them. In fact, they're here right now." (That had been the moment when the head FBI man had started waving his arms back and forth in a negative manner; Harrington remembered now his decision at that point not to mention to the woman that the call was being recorded. But weren't there court decisions to the effect that people *had* to be informed if their calls were being recorded?)

"You already called them."

"Well, it did seem the thing to do. Maurice said you people carried guns and seemed extremely menacing."

"All right, all right. We'll forget that part. The point is, you want your kid back, right?"

Slight hesitation. "Well, of course." (Listening to the tape now, Harrington could see where that hesitation might very easily be misconstrued. But he hadn't been thinking it *over*, or anything like that, it was merely that the question had been raised so suddenly it had startled him. Naturally he wanted Jimmy back, he was a fine lad, an excellent boy. There were times when Harrington wished he'd named this son Herbert, rather than having thrown the name away on his first son by his first marriage; the actual Herbert, now a twenty-eight-year-old hippie on a commune in Chad, had little to recommend him. In fact, nothing. In fact, it was good sound business sense on the kidnappers' part to steal Jimmy rather than Herbert Jr., since Harrington doubted very much he would *pay* one hundred fifty thousand dollars for the return of that clod.)

"All right. You want him back. But it will cost you."

"Yes, I'd rather thought it would. You people speak of that as the *ransom*, don't you?"

"What? Yeah, right, the ransom. That's what this call's all about."

"I thought as much."

"Yeah. Okay, here it is. Tomorrow, you get a hundred—" Clatter, clatter. "Damn it!"

"Beg pardon?"

"Hold on, I lost my—" Rattling sounds. "Just a minute, it's—" More rattling sounds. "Okay, here we go. Tomorrow, you get a hundred fifty thousand dollars in cash. In old—"

"I doubt I could go that high."

"—bills. You— What?"

"You say tomorrow. I take it time is of the essence here, and I'm not sure I could gather a hundred fifty thousand in cash in one day. I might be able to do eighty-five."

"Wait a minute, you're going ahead of me."

"I'm what?"

"Here it is. That's up to you. The longer it takes, the longer it'll be before you see your Buh—Jimmy again."

"Oh, I see, it isn't necessarily tomorrow."

"It's whenever you want him back, Buster." She was sounding really very irascible by this point.

"I was just thinking, if you wanted to complete this operation tomorrow, you might settle for eighty-five thousand."

"I said a hundred fifty thousand, and I meant a hundred fifty thousand. You think we're gonna *haggle*?"

"Certainly not. I'm not dickering over the well-being of my child, it's merely that I thought, within the time frame you appeared to be contem—"

"All right, all right, let it go. It's a hundred fifty thousand, no matter what."

"Very well." He sounded a bit chilly himself by this time, and listening to the recording now he could only applaud his decision then to let the woman see a bit of his irritation.

"Okay. We'll go over it again. Tomorrow you get— Well. As soon as you can, okay? As soon as you can, you get a hundred fifty thousand dollars in cash. In old bills. You pack it in a suitcase, and stay by your phone. I'll call again to give you the next instructions."

(It was during that statement of the woman's that the head FBI man had extended toward Harrington a slip of paper containing the pencilled words, "Tell her to prove it.")

"Um. Prove it."

"What?"

"I said, prove it."

"Prove what? That I'm gonna call you again?"

(During which, the head FBI man had been with great exaggeration mouthing the sentence, "That they have the kid!")

"No, um— Oh! That you have the kid. My son. Jimmy."

"Of course we have him, why would I call you if we didn't have him?"

"Well, I just want you to prove it, that's all."

"Prove it how? He isn't here by the phone."

"Well, I don't know how."

"Okay, look. Check this with the chauffeur. The Caddy was too wide for the truck. The planks broke. We all wore Mickey Mouse masks. We drove a blue Caprice. Okay?"

(The head FBI man had been nodding.) "That's fine."

"You're satisfied, huh?"

"Yes. Thank you very much."

"Yeah." It sounded very sour indeed. "I'll call you by four o'clock tomorrow afternoon."

"Well, there's a possibility—" (*click*) "—I'll be called to Washington tomorrow to appear before the SEC, but— Hello? Hello?" (away from the phone) "I believe she hung up."

"Okay," the head FBI man said. "Switch it off."

The tape technician switched it off.

The head FBI man said, "You recognize the voice?"

"I didn't recognize *either* voice," Harrington said. "Did that really sound like me?"

"Yeah, it sounded like you. But the other one didn't sound like anybody else you know, huh?"

"How could it?"

"Maybe a disgruntled former employee? A servant out here, somebody like that?"

"Well, she did sound disgruntled enough, I'll say that for her. But the voice doesn't ring any bells at all. I'm sorry."

The head FBI man shrugged. "Sometimes it pans out,"

104

he said. "Usually it don't." Nodding thoughtfully toward the tape machine, he said, "There's some interesting things in there."

"Really?"

"We didn't know it was a Caprice."

"A caprice? I'd call it something more serious than that."

"The kind of car," the head FBI man said. "Your chauffeur just said it was a blue car, so that's a piece of information we picked up."

"Oh, very good."

"And that slip of the tongue there. Be interesting to find out who this 'Bobby' is."

"Do you suppose they kidnapped more than one child today? Maybe they're making a whole raft of phone calls."

The head FBI man frowned, thinking that over. "Mass kidnappings?" He turned to one of the assistant FBI men who'd been hovering all evening in the corners of the room. "Look into that, Kirby," he said. "See do we have any more kidnapping reports today."

"Right." The assistant FBI man faded from the room, not like a person walking out of a room, but like a television picture fading from the screen when the power has been turned off.

"Another thing," the head FBI man said, turning back to Harrington. "It sounded at one point there like she was reading a prepared statement."

"Yes, I noticed that," Harrington said. "I think she lost her place for a minute there."

"Could be the kidnappers sent a dummy out to make the call, somebody that isn't really part of the gang. So if we traced the call and got her, she wouldn't be able to tell us anything."

"Very clever," Harrington said.

The head FBI man nodded. "We're up against a shrewd gang of professionals," he said, with a kind of gloomy satisfaction. "That'll make it tough to catch them. On the

105

other hand, it means the boy is probably safe. It's your amateurs that panic and start killing people; your professionals don't do that."

"It all seemed very professional to me, too," Harrington said. "Speaking as a layman, that is. But the truck, and the school bus, and so forth."

"Very carefully planned." The head FBI man stroked his craggy jaw. "I keep thinking I've seen that MO somewhere before," he said.

"MO?"

"Modus operandi. Method of operations."

"Isn't that interesting," Harrington said. "The way the initials work in both Latin and English."

"Yeah," the head FBI man said. "I'll have to run it through our computers down in Washington, see do we come up with something." He nodded thoughtfully, then became more brisk. "Now," he said, "about the payoff."

"Yes," Harrington said. "I was wondering about that."

"We'll try to recover your money, naturally," the head FBI man said. "We'll even try to set a trap with it if we can, though I think this bunch is probably too sharp for that."

"I got that impression," Harrington said.

"The main point is to recover the child. The money is secondary."

"Certainly."

The head FBI man nodded again, and said, "How long do you think it'll take to get the money together?"

"Well, it's too late to do anything tonight." Harrington frowned, considering the problem. "I'll call my accountant in the morning, work out the best way to handle this, from a variety of points of view. You may not be aware of this, but money paid to a kidnapper is not deductible on your income tax."

The head FBI man looked interested. "It isn't?"

"No. I remember running across that while looking up something for a client. I don't recall the justification; possibly it's considered payment for a service, non-business-connected."

"I've never had much to do over on the Treasury side," the head FBI man said.

"In any event, there are various ways of going about it. Sale of securities, depending on whether it would be long-term or short-term gains, possibly loans against my margin accounts where my portfolio has increased sufficiently in value, various possibilities. Well, I'll talk it over with Markham in the morning."

"But how long do you figure it'll take?"

"Really, you know," Harrington said, "the most difficult part is going to be conversion of assets to cash, actual paper money. I don't believe I know anyone who deals in cash."

"Banks do," the head FBI man said.

"Eh? Oh, of course! I never think of them that way."

"I still want to know how long. Two days? Three?"

"Oh, good Lord, no. I should have the liquidity by noon. One at the latest."

"Tomorrow?"

"Certainly tomorrow. Then it all depnds how long it takes to bring the currency out here."

"We'll take care of that," the head FBI man said. He was frowning deeply, studying Harrington's face. "Mr. Harrington," he said. "Can I ask you a question?"

"Of course."

"That business about the eighty-five thousand, that was all you could raise tomorrow. Do you mean you really *were* haggling?"

Harrington thought about it. In sudden surprise, he said, "Why, yes! I do believe I was."

The head FBI man looked at him. He didn't say anything.

"It was just force of habit," Harrington said. Then when the head FBI man continued to gaze at him unspeaking, he added, "I certainly wasn't going to turn the deal *down*."

107

18

AFTER DINNER, JIMMY went back to work. The fact that the boards were nailed to the outside of the window frames rather than the inside made his task a bit more difficult, but not impossible. He had removed one board before the cooking woman had brought him his dinner—how unearthly an adult wearing a Mickey Mouse mask could look in just the glow of a flashlight—and now he was removing more. They were fairly narrow boards, and he thought it likely he'd have to deal with four of them before making a space wide enough to climb out through.

His method was simple, but time-consuming. With the screwdriver, he would pry the board a bit loose, then oil the nails as he worked to keep them from squeaking. A bit at a time, prying and oiling, prying and oiling, he would loosen the board from the window frame. The final fraction was always the trickiest, since he didn't want the board to fall out onto the ground below; managing to avoid that, he would bring the board inside, then use the pliers to snap each nail off short. After oiling the nails once more, he would put the board back in place, the stubby nails slipping a short distance into their former seats in the window frame. The boards looked the same as before, but would pop out at the touch of a finger.

It was that last part that took the extra time. The job would have been much quicker and simpler if all he had to do was bash the boards out and depart. But in the first place he never knew when they might decide to come back up and double-check on him, and in the second place he wanted to leave them with a certain amount of misdirection and confusion. Therefore he took the extra time to do the job right, and considered it time well spent.

Outside, in those intervals when he had a board out of the window space, he could hear the rain continuing to pound. This room faced the back of the house, and there was no light outside at all, nothing but pitch blackness and the sound of pelting rain.

Some water did splash in from time to time, but not enough to give him away. A worse problem was the cold; a chill wet wind blew in whenever he had a board off the window, and his jacket just wasn't warm enough for weather like this. When he'd put it on this morning, the worst climate he'd expected to be exposed to was the air-conditioning in Dr. Schraubenzieher's office.

Well, one did have to expect to rough it from time to time in this life. With which thought Jimmy snapped the last nail that needed to be snapped, picked up the oilcan, oiled the nails in this fourth board, and carefully reinserted the board into the window, thus not only restoring the original appearance of the room, but also eliminating again that whistling wind.

What next? The tools and oilcan went into the toolbox, and the toolbox went into the space beneath the floorboard he had previously loosened. Flashing the light around the room, he reassured himself he wasn't leaving any unnecessary clues in his wake, and then turned to the rope.

It was quite long, but maybe not as thick or as strong as he would have liked it. Still, it would have to do, and once it was doubled it surely would do. Fine. So now there was nothing to do but depart.

So why did he hesitate? Why did he glance ruefully toward that small cot with its inadequate blankets?

Childishness, he told himself. Babyishness and weakness. And not to be given in to.

Taking a deep breath, squaring his shoulders, he hesitated just a second longer, then abruptly began to move, and from then on continued to move steadily and smoothly, doing everything just as he had planned it.

First, all four boards were taken out, and stacked next

to the window. Next, one end of the rope was slipped through between the still-attached fifth and sixth boards, in a tiny space showing down by the windowsill. That end of the rope was played through and around the outside of the fifth board and back into the room, until the center of the rope rested on the windowsill, against the bottom of the fifth board, inside the room. Dirt smudged on that length of rope made it virtually invisible.

Now. The two lengths of rope were allowed to hang down along the outer wall of the house. Jimmy, leaning out, feeling now the force of the wind and rain on his head, grasped the two lengths, brought a part of it back into the room, and tied a loop in it that would hang about three feet below the window. Then he dropped it outside again.

The rest would have to be done in darkness. Switching off the flashlight, Jimmy put it in his jacket pocket and felt his way to the window. Climbing carefully over the sill, he grasped the rope, pulled it up till he felt the loop, and put the loop like a stirrup over his right foot. Then he lowered himself slowly out of the window until he was standing on the loop of rope, his forearms resting on the windowsill.

Now for the tricky part. Reaching inside, he took the first board, which he knew belonged in position number four, and working by feel he slipped it back into place. Then three, and then two. Number one was the most difficult, since he had such a narrow space to bring the board out through, and he almost gave the whole thing up as an overelaboration, but at last he did get the thing out and in place, and felt better for having done it.

The idea was, whenever the gang next decided to check on him the room would appear to be unchanged. They would have to believe that he'd managed to turn the key in the lock from inside, and that while he was no longer in the room he must still be somewhere in the house. So they would confine their search, at least for a while, to the interior of the house, thus giving him longer to get away.

And if worse came to worst, if they did catch him again,

he would say that he'd turned the key with his ballpoint pen insert, had locked the door again behind himself, and had sneaked downstairs, going out the front door while they were all searching elsewhere. If they swallowed that and put him back in the same room—which they probably would, since they didn't have any other room prepared for him—he could simply take the boards down again and escape all over.

So. Having been as clever as possible in his departure, Jimmy now rappelled down the side of the house, permitting the back of his jacket to take most of the stress and most of the friction of the rope passing through, and all at once he found himself standing in mud, on the ground, outside the house.

Escape; he'd done it.

Now all that was left was to walk to the highway, hail a passing car, and inform the police. This gang would be rounded up, probably in less than an hour, and by midnight Jimmy would be safely at home and asleep in his own bed.

He almost felt sorry for the kidnappers. But they couldn't say they hadn't asked for it.

For the first leg of the journey he wouldn't be able to use the flashlight, and it really was dark out here. Also wet. Also cold. Already drenched to the skin, Jimmy reached out in front of himself, patted the weathered boards of the house, and then moved off to his right, keeping his left hand constantly in touch with the house.

Travelling that way, he walked around the house to the front, and there at last he did see some light; flickering yellowish light showing through chinks in the boarded-up living room windows. So, if he turned his back on those lights, the farm road should lead directly away in front of him. Turning that way, looking over his shoulder to be sure he was facing exactly away from the light, he made off cautiously into the rain-drenched darkness.

The first two times he looked over his shoulder those

faint lines of light were still there, but the third time they were gone. "Ten more steps," he whispered to himself, and made ten slow slithering steps through the mud before hesitantly switching on the flashlight, keeping his fingers closed over most of the glass so not too much light would come out.

He was in a field. At one time under cultivation, it had apparently come recently into a state of semi-abandonment. That is, no crop was grown here, but it seemed as though someone was keeping the rougher vegetation cut back, and any case, it wasn't a road.

To the left? Jimmy flashed the light that way, and couldn't see any road.

To the right? No.

Okay. So he'd have to do it differently; go back to the house and start all over, with quick on-offs of the flashlight right from the beginning, so he wouldn't get lost. Flashlight off, he turned around and headed back the way he'd come.

No house. After a while he became pretty sure he should have reached the house, and there just wasn't any house. No thin lines of yellow light at all, not a one.

Oh, the *hell* with this darkness! Switching on the flashlight, not putting any fingers over the glass at all, he aimed the beam all around himself, and didn't see a damn thing.

Where was the house? Where was the road?

It was getting cold out here. The rain didn't help and the wind didn't help, and even *without* them it would have been cold. With them, it was becoming almost terrifying.

Well, he couldn't just stand here. If he didn't get to someplace pretty soon, he'd be in big trouble. He could die of exposure out here, and wouldn't *that* be a dumb thing to do!

Apparently he'd come farther from the house than he'd thought. It had to be out in front of him, invisible in the pounding rain. So the thing to do was keep moving forward.

112

He moved forward. His shoes were becoming heavy with mud, and after a while it became easier to just drag his feet through the puddles rather than try to lift them.

Heavy. Cold. Hard to see in this light. And now the flashlight was starting to dim.

A road.

He didn't believe it. He almost walked across it and off the other side, except that his sliding foot got caught briefly in one of the ruts. He looked down to see what the problem was, saw the parallel lines going from left to right, and shone the dimming light off to his right. A definite road, a farm road, two deep ruts with a grassy lane in the center.

Which way? He had to have overshot the house somehow, so it would be off to the left there. The highway would be to the right, so that's the direction he took.

It was easier walking now, on the high grassy mound between the ruts. He made good time, all things considered, and he just didn't believe it when he saw those yellow lines of light out in the darkness ahead of himself and to the right, just outside the yellow cone from the flashlight.

The house.

He could see the way it went now. The road didn't go directly to the house, it came in from an angle and swept across in front of it. His ideas of his location and direction had been wrong at every single stage of the journey.

So the highway was back the other way. Jimmy turned and shone his feeble light down the road he'd just some along. He looked back over his shoulder at the house.

He sighed.

113

19

A LUMINOUS AFTERNOON in the black-and-white forest. The monster, played by Boris Karloff, pauses as he hears the sweet notes of a violin. His face lights, he lumbers through the woods, following the sound. He comes to a cosy cottage amid the trees, very gingerbread. Inside, the violin is being played by a blind hermit, who is being played by O. P. Heggie. The monster approaches, and pounds on the door.

Someone pounded on the door.

"Eee! " Murch's Mom said, and jumped straight up out of her folding chair. Which folded, and fell over with a slap.

They had all been sitting around the battery-operated small television set they'd brought out to follow the kidnapping news. There's been no kidnapping news—apparently the cops were keeping a news blackout on—so now they were watching the late movie. The three kerosene lamps, the hibachi in the fireplace, and the flickering television screen, all gave some light and less heat.

Someone pounded at the door again. On the TV screen, the blind hermit opened his door to the monster.

The others had all scrambled to their feet too by now, though without knocking over their chairs. Harshly Kelp whispered, "What do we do?"

"They know we're here," Dortmunder said. "Let me do the talking." He glanced upstairs, and said, "May, if the kid acts up, say something about him having nightmares and go up there and keep him quiet."

May nodded. The pounding sounded at the door for a third time. Murch's Mom said, "I'll go."

They all waited. Dortmunder's hand was near the pocket

114

with his revolver. Murch's Mom opened the door and said, "Well, for God—"

And the kid walked in.

"Holy Toledo! " Murch said.

Kelp, slapping his hands to his face, yelled, "Masks! Masks! Don't let him see your faces! "

Dortmunder didn't believe it. He stared at the kid, looking as wet and muddy and ragged as a drowned kitten, and then he looked upstairs. And then he *ran* upstairs. He didn't know what he thought, maybe that the kid was twins or something, but he just didn't believe he wasn't in that room.

The door was locked, and Dortmunder fumbled with the key for a few seconds before remembering he had a flashlight in his other pocket—the pocket without the revolver in it—but once he had the flashlight out and shining he swiftly unlocked the door, pushed it open, stepped inside, aimed the light beam all around, and the room was empty.

Empty. How could that be? Dortmunder looked under the bed and in the closet, and the kid was gone.

But the door had been locked. The boards were still on the windows. There were no holes in the ceiling or the floor or any of the walls. There were no other exits from the room.

"It's a locked-room mystery," Dortmunder told himself, and stood in the middle of the room, flashing the light slowly this way and that, completely baffled.

Downstairs, Kelp was the first one to find and don his mask, and then he ran over to grab the kid. "I'm not trying to get away," the kid said. "I'm just closing the door."

"Well, just stay put," Kelp told him.

"I came back, didn't I? Why should I try to get away?"

May too had put on her mask by now, and she came over to say, "You're drenched! You'll catch your death! You've got to get out of those wet clothes right now." To Kelp she said, "Go up and get his blankets," and to the boy she said, "Now get out of those clothes."

Hearing the authoritarian maternal voice, both Kelp and the kid promptly obeyed. Meantime, Murch and his Mom were squabbling over the mask they'd both been using. Murch's Mom hadn't worn one during the kidnapping, and when she'd gone upstairs with May earlier she'd borrowed her son's. It hadn't been anticipated the whole gang would be in the boy's presence at once. Now they were both holding the mask, and tugging a little. "Stan," Murch's Mom said, "you give me that. I have a much more memorable face than you."

"You do not, Mom, you look like every other cabdriver in New York. I really *need* that mask, and anyway it's mine."

Going upstairs, Kelp found Dortmunder in the kid's room, walking around in circles, shining his flashlight here and there. Kelp said, "What are you doing?"

"It's impossible," Dortmunder said. "How'd he get out?"

"I dunno." Kelp picked up the blankets and the pyjamas from the bed. "Why don't you ask him?"

"He must of walked through the wall," Dortmunder said.

Kelp went out, leaving Dortmunder still making circles, and hurried downstairs. May had the boy over by the fireplace now, where there was still some heat from the charcoal in the hibachi. She had him stripped down to his underpants, and she immediately began rubbing him down with one of the blankets, using it as a towel. "You're really wet," she said. "You're really wet."

"And cold," the boy said. 'It's no-fooling cold out there." He yawned.

On the other side of the room, Murch's Mom was triumphantly wearing the Murch family Mickey Mouse mask. Murch, showing his irritation by the set of his shoulders, sat at the card table with his elbows on the table and his hands over his face. Lantern light glinted on his eyes as he peered between his fingers.

116

Dortmunder came downstairs. He marched across the living room to where May was drying the boy with a blanket, glowered down at him, and said, "All right, kid. How'd you do it?"

May, on one knee in front of the boy, folded him in her arms, glared up at Dortmunder, and said, "Don't you strike this child."

"What strike? I wanna know how he got out of the goddam room."

Kelp whispered with harsh urgency. "Your mask! Your mask!"

Dortmunder looked around. "What?" Then he felt his bare face and said, "Oh, for Christ's sake." His mask was near him, on the mantel, and when he picked it up it was warm from hibachi heat. He pulled it angrily over his head and said, "It stinks worse when it's hot."

May said, "You men get some wood, build a real fire in this fireplace. We need some heat in this room."

"What wood?" Dortmunder said. "Everything outside'll be too wet to burn."

"There must be wood in here," she said. "Something to make a fire."

"All right," Dortmunder said, looking around. "All right, I'll find something."

"I can't help," Murch said. His voice was muffled by his hands, so that he sounded as though he too had a mask on. "I can't very well carry wood with my hands over my face," he said, and even through the muffling effect the tone of grievance could be heard in his voice.

"So you'll sit there," his Mom told him.

Dortmunder and Kelp went out to the kitchen, where they found some built-in shelving they could rip out, and for a time the empty house echoed with ripping, rending, crashing sounds from the kitchen. Meantime, Murch's Mom moved the hibachi to a corner of the fireplace and made a bed for the fire out of ripped-up pieces of cardboard from the cartons that had contained their provi-

117

sions. Murch sat at the card table and watched the action through his fingers, and May dressed the boy in pyjamas and wrapped the other blanket around him. On the television screen, which no one was watching, the blind hermit was playing his violin for the monster.

Dortmunder and Kelp brought a lot of jagged pieces of wood in, stacked them in the fireplace, and lit the cardboard underneath. The fire started up at once, and smoked terrifically for half a minute, during which time everybody coughed and waved their arms and shouted unintelligible and unfollowable orders about the flue. Then all at once the chimney began to draw, the fire flared up, the smoke was sucked away into the rain and the wind outside, and heat wafted out across the room.

"That's nice," May said.

Jimmy, warm now and dry, turned at last and noticed the television set. "Oh!" he said. "*Bride of Frankenstein*! There's some beautiful shots in that. It was directed by James Whale, you know, he also did the original *Frankenstein* and *The Invisible Man*. Just incredible camera angles. Can I watch?"

"It's past your bedtime," May said.

"Oh, that can't count *now*," Jimmy said. "Besides, my room is cold, and you want to keep me warm, don't you?"

"An exercise-yard lawyer," Dortmunder said.

Murch said, "Put the kid upstairs, will you? I don't want to spend the rest of my life with my hands over my face."

Dortmunder said, "And I don't want to keep this goddam mask on any more."

Jimmy said, "I'll make you a deal."

They all looked at him. Murch's Mom said, "You'll make us a what?"

"I already saw your faces anyway," Jimmy said, "when I first came in. But if you let me stay and watch the movie, you can take your masks off and I promise I'll make believe you kept them on. I'll never identify you, and I won't tell the police or anybody else that I ever saw you or that I know what you look like. I'll make a solemn vow." He held his right hand up in the three-finger Boy Scout oath sign, though he was not now and never had been a Boy Scout. But he meant it just the same.

The gang all looked at one another. Murch's Mom said, "Well, it would be easier."

Kelp said, "But that's not the way it's done. That's not the way it's *done*."

Dortmunder said, "You mean in that goddam book?"

"I mean anywhere. But, all right, in the book. Could you imagine the gang in that book taking their masks off and sitting down with the victim and watch *Bride of Frankenstein*?"

"I really really promise," Jimmy said.

Dortmunder yanked his mask off and threw it into a corner. "I'll take the kid's word for it," he said.

"So do I," said Murch's Mom, and pulled her own mask off. "This thing flattens my hair anyway."

Murch took his hands down from his face. "Boy, that's a strain on the arms," he said.

May took off her mask, looked at it, and said, "I always thought this thing was pretty silly anyway."

Kelp, the only one in the room with a Mickey Mouse mask on, said, "You people don't seem to understand. If you don't do a thing right, how do you expect to get away with anything?"

"Be quiet," Murch's Mom said. "I'm watching the movie."

May said to Jimmy, "Come here, sit with me."

"I'm a little old for sitting on people's laps," Jimmy said.

"Okay," May said. "Then I'll sit on yours."

Jimmy laughed. "You win," he said. "I'll sit on your lap."

They all arranged themselves in their chairs before the television set again, as they had been before Jimmy had come back. Kelp looked at them all, looked at the kid, looked at the TV, shook his Mickey Mouse-masked head, shrugged, pulled the mask off, flipped it away, and sat down to watch the movie.

The hermit and the monster ate dinner together. "Food good," said the monster. The hermit gave him a cigar.

20

WHEN DORTMUNDER WOKE up he was stiff as a board. He sat up, creaking in every joint, and discovered that his air mattress had developed a leak during the night. In order to have something for them to sleep on, without having to cart half a dozen beds out here from New York, Murch and his Mom had bought a bunch of inflatable air mattresses, the kind that people use in their swimming pools. And Dortmunder's had sprung a leak during the night, lowering him slowly to the dining room floor, on which he had done the rest of his sleeping. The result being that he was now so stiff he could barely move.

Grey-white daylight crept through the boarded windows, showing him the empty room, the black hole in the center of the ceiling where a chandelier had been removed, and the other two air mattresses. Murch's was empty, but a blanketed mound breathed slowly and evenly on the other one; Dortmunder felt fatalistic irritation at that. Kelp's air mattress had *not* leaked, he was over there sleeping like a baby.

Last night, after the movie, the kid had been put back up in his room with the door locked, for whatever good it might do. But he'd been asleep by then—Dortmunder had had to carry him upstairs—so maybe he was still around. In any event, mattresses had been blown up for the ladies in the living room and for the gentlemen next door in the dining room, and to the pitter-pat of rain on the floor—the roof leaked—they had all gone off to sleep.

Speaking of pitter-pat, there wasn't any. Dortmunder frowned at the windows, but the boards were too close together for him to see out or even to tell what kind of day it was; though this light did seem too pale to be direct sunshine. Anyway, the rain had apparently stopped.

Well, there was nothing for it but to get up, or at least to make the attempt. Also, there was the smell of coffee in the air, which made Dortmunder's stomach growl softly to itself in anticipation. Last night's Lurps had been better than nothing, but they weren't exactly the kind of meal he was used to.

"Um," he said, when he leaned forward, and, "Oof," when he stretched one hand out on the floor and shifted his weight over onto it. "Aggghh," he said, when he heaved his body heavily over onto one knee, and, "Oh, Jee-sus," when at last he struggled to his feet.

What a back. It felt as though somebody had pounded a lot of finishing nails into it last night. He bent, twisted, arched his back, and listened to his body creak and snap and complain. Moving a lot like Boris Karloff in that movie last night—in fact, he looked a bit like that character—he staggered out of the dining room and into the living room, where he found May, Murch's Mom and the kid sitting at the card table, playing hearts. May said, "Good morning. There's hot water on the hibachi, if you want to make yourself some coffee."

"I don't want to make myself some coffee," Dortmunder said. "My mattress leaked, I slept on the floor, I'm too stiff to bend over."

"In other words," May said, "you want me to make it."

"That's right," Dortmunder said.

"After this hand," May said.

Dortmunder grunted, and went over to open the door and look out at the world. The sky was very grey and

121

the ground was very wet and there was still a damp chill in the air.

"Shut that door," Murch's Mom called. "It's nice and warm in here, let's keep it that way."

Dortmunder shut the door. "Where's Stan?" he said.

Murch's Mom said, "He went to get some groceries."

"Groceries?"

May said, "Jimmy says he's an expert at scrambled eggs."

"I always make my own breakfast," Jimmy said. "Mrs. Engelberg is hopeless." Looking slyly at Murch's Mom he said. "You wouldn't be shooting the moon, would you?"

"Of course not," Murch's Mom said. "With this hand?"

Dortmunder walked slowly around the room, bending this way and that, shrugging his shoulders, twisting his head around. Everything hurt. His *wrists* hurt. He said, "Isn't that hand over?"

"Not quite," Murch's Mom said.

Dortmunder went over and looked at the hand. They each had two cards left and it was Murch's Mom's lead. Dortmunder, kibitzing over her shoulder, saw that she had the ace of clubs and the ten of diamonds left. "Well, I might as well get rid of my last winner," she said, and tossed out the ace of clubs.

Dortmunder walked around to kibitz May's hand, while Jimmy said, "I thought you weren't shooting the moon."

"I'm not," Murch's Mom said. "I just don't want to get stuck with the last lead."

"Sure," Jimmy said.

May had to play second, on Murch's Mom's ace of clubs, and she had the ace of hearts and the jack of diamonds. Dortmunder watched May's hand hover over the jack of diamonds, which would beat Murch's Mom's final ten of diamonds lead, then hover over the ace of hearts. Then it hovered over the jack of diamonds again. Then the ace of hearts again.

Dortmunder's stomach growled. Loudly.

"Oh, all right," May said, and threw the jack of diamonds, holding back the ace of hearts.

"I didn't say anything," Dortmunder said.

"Your stomach did," May told him.

"I can't help that." Dortmunder went on around the table to look at Jimmy's hand. The kid had the king of hearts and the queen of diamonds, and he barely hesitated at all before throwing the king of hearts. "If you want to shoot the moon," he said, "I might as well help."

Murch's Mom, drawing in the trick, looked at the kid with sudden sharp suspicion. "What have you done, you bad boy?" she asked, and tossed out the ten of diamonds.

"Oh, dear," May said, and dropped the ace of hearts on it.

"I kept a stopper," Jimmy said calmly. He dropped the queen of diamonds and said, "That's twenty-five for you and one for me."

"And coffee for me," Dortmunder said.

"Yes yes," May said.

Murch's Mom, who was well-known as a poor loser, wrote down the scores and said, "You think you're pretty cute, don't you?"

"I've learned over the course of years," Jimmy told her, "that defensive play is much more profitable in the long run."

"The course of *years*? Are you kidding me?"

His face as innocent as a choirboy's, Jimmy said, "What's the score, anyway?"

Murch's Mom tossed the pad across the table to him. "Read it yourself," she said.

Dortmunder got his coffee from May, who then went back to her game. Dortmunder walked around and around, drinking coffee and trying to limber up, and after a while Murch came in, with eggs and milk and butter and bread and a newspaper and a frying pan and a pale blue flight bag that said *Air France* on it and God knows what else. Dortmunder said, "We gonna *live* here?"

Murch's Mom said, "There's things we need. Don't complain all the time."

Dortmunder said, "What's with the Air France bag?"

May was pulling clothing out of it: sweater, socks, trousers, all boy-size. "Jimmy doesn't have anything to wear," she said. "It's too cold for what he had on, and that's all dirty now anyway."

Murch said to Jimmy, "I'm sorry, kid, they didn't have an avocado."

"That's okay," Jimmy said. "We can make a fine salad without it."

Dortmunder said, "Avocado?" Things, it seemed to him, were getting out of hand: Air France bags, avocados. However, nobody else in this room seemed to think things were getting out of hand, and he knew better than to raise the question with any of them, so he went back to the dining room.

Where Kelp was wide awake, sitting up, reading *Child Heist*. "Morning," Kelp said, grinning from ear to ear. "I slept like a top. How about you?"

"Like a bottom," Dortmunder told him. "My mattress leaked."

"Oh, that's a shame."

"Don't you ever get tired of that book?"

"Well, we got the money switch coming up this afternoon," Kelp said. "I thought I ought to refresh my memory, read that chapter again. You oughta take a look at it, too."

"Oh, yeah?"

"Absolutely," Kelp said. "Chapter twelve. Page a hundred and nine."

21

CHAPTER TWELVE

At exactly four P.M. Ruth, in a pay phone at a Shell station in Patchogue, Long Island, made the second call.

"Myers residence."

"Let me talk to George Myers."

"Who's calling, please?"

"Tell him," Ruth said, "it's the people who have his kid."

"One moment, please."

But it was only fifteen or twenty seconds before Myers was on the phone, saying, "How's Bobby? Is he all right?"

"He's fine," Ruth said. "You've got the money?"

"Yes. Can't I speak to him?"

"He isn't here. You do right, you'll have him back tonight."

"I'll do what you say, don't worry about that."

"I'm not the one has to worry," Ruth said. "I want you to get into your car with the money. Use the Lincoln. You can bring your chauffeur along, but nobody else."

"All right," Myers said. "All right."

"Drive over to Northern State Parkway," Ruth told him, "and get up on the eastbound. Drive at a steady fifty. We'll meet you along the way."

"Yes," Myers said. "All right."

"Do it now," Ruth said, and hung up. Going outside, she got into the Pinto, drove away from the Shell station, and headed for the other phone booth.

Northward, a block from the Myers estate, Parker and Krauss sat in the Dodge and waited. Henley and Angie were back at the farmhouse, watching the kid.

"Here he comes," Krauss said.

They watched the Lincoln go by, the chauffeur driving, Myers hunched forward nervously on the back seat. When it was two blocks away, Krauss started the Dodge, and they moved off in its wake.

After a few blocks Parker said, "He's going the right way. And there's nobody else with him."

"Right. There's a phone in this drugstore up here."

They let the Lincoln go on, heading for Northern State Parkway. While Krauss stayed in the car, Parker went into the drugstore and called Ruth at the other pay phone. She had just arrived, and picked it up on the first ring. "Yes?"

"He's on his way," Parker said. "He'll be taking the ramp in maybe two minutes."

Ruth checked her watch, "Right," she said.

Parker got back into the Dodge, and Krauss took off again in the wake of the Lincoln, which was no longer in sight. They entered the parkway, Krauss lifted them to sixty-five, and soon they passed the Lincoln, moving obediently at fifty in the right lane. In the back seat, Myers was still hunching forward.

In the phone booth, Ruth dialled the operator, and told her, "I want to call a mobile unit in a private car."

"Do you have the number?"

"Yes, I do."

Krauss reached their exit, took the off ramp, looped around under the parkway, and stopped next to the wall of the overpass. They'd chosen this exit with care, it having no nearby buildings or population. Potato fields stretched away flat and dry in all directions, with stands of trees in the distance. To the south the secondary road led to the first fringes of a town, but northward there were merely trees and the black top curving away out of sight.

In the limousine moving along the parkway like a slow black whale amid darting dolphins, George Myers leaned forward in his seat, staring at the road ahead, wondering when and how they would contact him. The suitcase full of money was on the seat beside him. Albert Judson, the chauffeur, kept his eyes on the road and the pace of the car at a steady fifty.

126

The telephone rang.

For the first few seconds, Myers was too disoriented to realize what that sound was. His concentration had been too exclusively outside the car, out ahead of him where the kidnappers were waiting. Now, startled, he looked quickly around, then suddenly understood. That's why they wanted him to use the Lincoln; they intended to phone him.

He picked up the receiver, almost afraid of the black plastic. Tentatively, he held it to his face. "Hello?"

"Myers?" It was the same woman's voice, cold and impersonal, with a tinge of roughness.

"Yes," he said. "I know who you are."

"Tell your chauffeur to stop at mile marker eighty-seven. At the small green sign. You'll find a milk bottle there with a piece of paper in it. That will give you your instructions."

"Yes, I will. But when—"

She had hung up. Myers held the phone a second longer, anxious, frustrated, then leaned forward again, saying, "Albert."

The chauffeur slightly turned his head, offering an ear. "Sir?"

Myers cradled the telephone. "We're to stop at mile marker eighty-seven," he said.

"Yes, sir." And, a second later, "There's number eighty-six."

Myers watched the small green sign go by, then looked forward again.

It was a long mile, but at the end of it the chauffeur eased the Lincoln off onto the gravel and came to a smooth stop next to the sign with the cream numerals 87 on it. "Wait, Albert," Myers said, and climbed from the car.

The milk bottle, looking like any piece of rubbish littering the edge of the highway, was on its side next to the sign. Picking it up, Myers fished the scrap of paper out of it, then tossed the bottle away and read the instructions:

Stop at next overpass. Drop suitcase on far verge of road below. Drive on.

Myers got back into the car. "We have to stop again at the next overpass," he said.

"Yes, sir."

The chauffeur eased them back out amid the traffic, and now drove even more slowly than before, waiting for the overpass.

It was less than a mile later, just beyond an exit ramp. The chauffeur stopped the limousine on the gravel again and Myers got out, this time carrying the suitcase. Looking around, hearing the *whish whish whish* of traffic hurrying by, he wondered if the police were living up to their promise. They'd assured him they wouldn't try to interfere with the money transfer in any way, wouldn't try to set any traps. "Let's get Bobby back first," one of them had said, "and then we'll go after the kidnappers." That was the way Myers felt, too, and the condition he would have in any event insisted on. But was it possible they'd been lying to him? Could some of these other cars rushing by him contain plainclothes policemen?

But all he had now was hope: the hope that he could trust the kidnappers, the hope that he could trust the police. Turning, he walked to the concrete railing of the overpass, looked over, and saw no one down below. The far verge was to his left. He walked that way, hoisted the suitcase onto the railing, and let it drop. He saw it hit the ground down there, amid the weeds, and then he turned and walked heavily back to the Lincoln.

Down below, Parker got out of the Dodge. A little dust settled where the suitcase had landed. No traffic came down the ramp, nothing moved anywhere. Parker walked swiftly back, picked up the suitcase, carried it to the car. Krauss was shifting into drive as Parker got into the seat beside him.

22

AT EXACTLY FIVE minutes after four Murch's Mom, in a pay phone at a Mobil station in Netcong, New Jersey, made the second call.

"Hello?"

"Let me talk to Herbert Harrington."

"Speaking."

"What?"

"This is Herbert Harrington speaking," the voice said in her ear. "Aren't you the kidnapper?"

"Wait a second," Murch's Mom said. She was trying to turn the page of a paperback book one-handed.

"Oh, dear," the voice said. "Have I made a mistake? I'm expecting a call from a kidnapper, and—"

"Yeah yeah," Murch's Mom said, "that's me, it's me, only hold on a second. *There!*"

"I beg your pardon?"

"Do you have the money?"

"Yes," Harrington said. "Yes, I do. I want you to know it wasn't easy to assemble that much cash in so short a period of time. If I didn't have some personal friends at Chase Manhattan, in fact, I don't believe it could have been done."

"But you've got it," Murch's Mom said.

"Yes, I do. In a small suitcase. I do have a question on that."

Murch's Mom frowned, scrinching her face up. Why couldn't it ever go smooth and simple, like in the book? "What kind of question?"

"This suitcase," Harrington said. "It cost forty-two eighty-four, with the tax. Now, should that come out of the hundred fifty thousand, or is that to be considered my expense?"

"What?"

"Please don't think I'm being difficult," Harrington said. "I've never handled a negotiation like this before, and I simply don't know what's considered normal practice."

Shaking her head, Murch's Mom said, "You pay for the suitcase. We don't pay for it, you pay for it." She was thinking, *There's nothing cheaper than a rich person.*

"Fine, fine," Harrington said. "I merely wanted to know."

"Okay," Murch's Mom said. "Can we get on with it?"

"Certainly."

"I want you to get into your car with the money," Murch's Mom read. "Use the Lincoln. You can—"

"What was that?"

Murch's Mom gave an exasperated sigh. "Now what?"

"Did you say a Lincoln? I don't have a—"

"The Cadillac!" She'd meant to make a pencil change to that effect, and she'd forgot. "I meant the Cadillac."

"Yes. Well, that's the only automobile I have."

Murch's Mom gritted her teeth. "So that's the one you'll use," she said, and this time she was thinking, *If I could get my hands on him, I'd strangle him.*

"Very well," Harrington said. "Am I to meet you somewhere?"

"Let's not rush me," Murch's Mom said. "So you'll use the Cadillac. You can bring your chauffeur along, but—"

"Well, I should think so," Harrington said. "I don't drive."

Murch's Mom was completely speechless. She had never in her life met anybody who didn't drive. She had been a cabdriver herself for a hundred years. Her boy Stan was *always* either in a car, driving it, or under a car, fixing it. Not drive? It was like not walking.

Harrington said, "Hello? Are you there?"

"I'm here. Why don't you drive? Is it some religious thing or something?"

"Why, no. I've simply never felt the need. I've always had a chauffeur. And in the city, of course, one takes cabs."

"Cabs," Murch's Mom said.

"They're perfectly satisfactory," Harrington said. "Except that recently, to tell the truth, I think the quality of the drivers has gone down."

"You're absolutely right!" Murch's Mom stood up straighter in the phone booth, and even jabbed the air with her finger two or three times, to emphasize a point. "It was the Seventy-one contract," she said. "It was a sellout to the owners, it screwed the cabby and the riding public both."

"Oh, is that the time the fare went up so drastically?"

"That's right," Murch's Mom said. "But I'm not talking about the fare, that was realistic, your New York City cabdriver had not been keeping up with inflation. It was a big jump, but it was just to get the cabby up where he *used* to be."

"It seemed a large leap somehow, almost double or something. I did notice it at the time."

"But where the cabby was screwed," Murch's Mom said, "*and* where the riding public was screwed, was in the split. They changed the formula on the split."

"I'm afraid I don't understand."

Murch's Mom was only too happy to explain; this whole union problem was a big hobbyhorse with her. "You work for a fleet owner," she said, "you split the meter take with him. You get maybe fifty-two percent, fifty-five, whatever."

"Yes, I see. And they changed the split?"

"They changed the *formula*," Murch's Mom said. "They fixed it so the owner has to give a bigger percent to a driver with more seniority."

"But surely that's only right. After all, if a man drives a cab for years and years, he—"

131

"But that's not what *happens*," Murch's Mom said. "What happens is, if the owner pulls in some bum off the street, can't find his way to the Empire State Building, gives him a job, puts him in a cab, the owner gets to keep a higher percentage of the meter!"

"Oh!" Harrington said. "I see what you mean; the contract makes it more advantageous to the owner to hire inexperienced drivers."

"Absolutely," Murch's Mom said. "So that's why you had all them potheads, them beatniks, driving around, playing cabdriver."

"I did have one last summer," Harrington said, "who didn't know his left from his right. At first I thought it was only because he didn't speak English, but in fact he didn't know left from right in *any* language. It's very hard to give travel directions to someone who doesn't know his left from his right."

Northward, a block from the Harrington estate, Dortmunder and Murch sat in a freshly stolen Mustang and waited. And waited. Murch said, "Shouldn't he come out pretty soon?"

"Yeah, he should," Dortmunder said.

"I wonder what he's doing," Murch said.

He was talking taxis with Murch's Mom. They were trading horror stories—the hippie driver fresh from Boston who didn't know there was a section of the city called Queens, the Oriental who didn't speak English and who drove at twelve miles an hour to the wrong airport—until finally it was Harrington who said, "But I'm sorry, I've changed the subject. I do apologize. We were talking about the ransom."

"Oh, yeah," Murch's Mom said. She looked at her watch, and it was almost quarter after four. "Right. Okay, let me start again. You'll get in the Cadillac with your chauffeur, but no other passengers."

"Yes."

"You'll drive to Interstate 80, and get up on it westbound. Drive at a steady fifty. We'll meet you along the way."

"Where?"

Murch's Mom frowned again. "What?"

"You'll meet me where along the way?"

"I don't tell you that now. You just get up there, and we'll contact you."

"But I don't understand. Where is it I'm going? What's my destination?"

"You just get on 80," Murch's Mom told him, "and travel west at fifty miles an hour. That's all you do, and we'll take over from there." The sense of camaraderie she'd felt with him over the issue of New York taxicabs had vanished; once again, what she really wanted to do was wring his neck.

"I've never heard of such a thing," Harrington said. "No destination. I don't know *anyone* who travels that way."

"Just do it," Murch's Mom said, and hung up in exasperation. Going outside, she got into the Roadrunner her son had stolen for her this morning, and headed for the other phone booth. She had originally objected to this move, saying she didn't see why she couldn't make both calls from the same booth, but Kelp had showed her where in *Child Heist* it was explained the cops might be tracing the first call, and might show up pretty soon at the phone both where the call was made. So okay, she'd go to the other phone booth.

Northward, Dortmunder and Murch continued to sit in the Mustang and wait. Murch said, "Do we have the number of the phone booth where Mom makes her first call?"

"No. Why should we?"

"I thought we could call her, see if anything went wrong."

"The smart guy that wrote the book," Dortmunder said, "didn't say anything about that."

On the Harrington estate, Herbert Harrington stood beside his Cadillac and argued with the head FBI man. "I don't see," he said, "why I can't have my own chauffeur. I *like* the way he drives."

"Kirby's a good driver," the head FBI man said. He was being patient in a way to show how impatient he really was. "And he's along just in case anything happens. Like they decide to kidnap you, too."

"Now, why on earth would they kidnap *me*? Who'd pay the ransom?"

"Your wife," the head FBI man said.

"My what? Oh, Claire! Hah, what a thought! *She* doesn't even know Jimmy's been stolen. She won't answer my calls."

"For your own protection," the head FBI man said, "we're going to insist that Kirby drive you. Believe me, he's a competent driver, he'll bring you back safe and sound."

Harrington frowned at the man in the front seat of the Cadillac, sitting there with Maurice's hat on his head. The hat was too large. "His hat is too large," Harrington said.

"It doesn't matter." The head FBI man held the door open. "You ought to get moving now, Mr. Harrington."

"I just don't like anything about this," Harrington said, and reluctantly slid into the back of the car. The suitcase full of money and his attaché case with some business papers were already in there, on the floor.

The head FBI man shut the door, perhaps a trifle more emphatically than necessary. "Okay, Kirby," he said, and the Cadillac slid forward over the white gravel of the driveway.

"Son of a gun," Murch said. "Here it comes."

"Damned if it doesn't," Dortmunder said.

The silver-grey Cadillac came purring around the curving blacktop road, scattering dead leaves in its wake. The right car: WAX 361, whip antenna. The chauffeur was at the wheel, and the father was in the back seat. As it was disappearing around the far curve—there were no straight

134

streets in this wealthy section of New Jersey—Murch started the Mustang, and they moved off in its wake.

It was two miles to Interstate 80. While Murch and Dortmunder hung well back, Kirby steered the big car around the bends and through the dales. It was fun driving a Caddy; maybe on the way back he could really open it up.

In the back seat, Harrington picked up his attaché case, opened it on the seat beside him, and riffled through the sheaves of documents. He hadn't been able to get to the office at all today, naturally, with all this mess going on, and the work was piling up. He picked up the phone and called his office in the city; his secretary had already been alerted to expect a late-afternoon call. At least he'd be able to get some of this accumulation cleared away during the drive.

Murch's Mom reached the other phone booth. It was next to a Burger King on route 46. She parked the Road-runner and went over to stand in the booth and wait. Outside, a group of juvenile delinquents showed up on motorcycles.

The Cadillac reached Interstate 80. Murch stopped at a Chevron station by the on ramp and Dortmunder phoned Murch's Mom at the other phone booth. When she answered, there was such a loud buzzing noise, hoarse and raspy, that he could barely hear her. "You got trouble on your line," he said.

She said, "What?"

"You got trouble on your line!"

"I can't hear you with all these stinking motorcycles!"

"Oh. *He's up on 80!*"

"*Right!*"

Dortmunder got back into the Mustang, and Murch took off again in the wake of the Cadillac. They went up on the Interstate, Murch put the Mustang up to sixty-eight, and soon they passed the Caddy, moving obediently at fifty in

135

the right lane. "Mom's already talking to him," Murch said.

They could see the father on the phone in back. The chauffeur glanced at them out of his reflecting sunglasses as they went by. *Look at that Mustang*, Kirby thought, and hated the frustration that he couldn't lean into this Caddy and run a couple rings about that little beast. Later; on the way back.

At the Burger King, Murch's Mom dialled the operator, and yelled, *"I want to call a mobile unit in a private car!"*

"Well, you don't have to yell about it," the operator said.

"What?"

"You have trouble on your line," the operator said. "Hang up and dial again."

"What? I can't hear you with all these motorcycles!"

"Oh," said the operator. "You want to call a mobile unit?"

"What?"

"Do you want to call a mobile unit?"

"Why do you think I'm putting up with all this?"

"Do you have the number?"

"Yes!"

Harrington was saying. "Now in the matter of that prospectus. I think our posture before the SEC is that while the prospectus did speak of *home* sites, it does not at any point say anything about a *community*. A community would necessarily imply the existence of available water. A home site would not. Country retreat, weekend cottage, that sort of thing. Have Bill Timmins see what he can root up by way of precedents."

"Yes, sir," said the secretary.

"Then call Danforth in Oklahoma and tell him that Marseilles crowd just will not budge on the three-for-two stock swap. Tell him my suggestion is that we threaten to simply bow out on the railroad end of it and carry our venture capital elsewhere. If he approves, try and arrange a phone

136

conference with Grandin for nine-thirty tomorrow morning, New York time. If Danforth has a problem, give him my home number, and tell him I should be there in, oh, two hours at the very most."

"Yes, sir," said the secretary.

"But the line's busy!" the operator said.

"Well, try again!" Murch's Mom said.

Murch reached the off ramp for the Hope exit, and slowed for the curve. In all of New Jersey, this was the closest Interstate 80 exit to the one described in the book. There was one small commercial building down on the county road, just north of the off ramp, but that was all. As for a main highway exit with *no* buildings or population around it, there was no such thing on Interstate 80 in New Jersey, and Dortmunder doubted there was any such thing along Northern State Parkway on Long Island, the site of *Child Heist*. The writer had just been making things easy for himself, that's all.

Murch pulled to a stop next to the wall of the overpass. Interstate 80 made a humming roof over their heads. "It won't be long now," Murch said.

Dortmunder didn't say anything.

"The line's still busy!" the operator said.

"Hold on a minute!"

"What?"

"I said hold on! Wait! Don't go away!"

"Oh!"

Murch's Mom, leaving the phone off the hook, stepped out of the booth and went over to the Roadrunner. She had seen tools on the back seat; yes, there was a nice big monkey wrench. She picked it up, hefted it, and went over to stand in front of the motorcyclists, who were sitting on their throbbing machines, filling their faces with whoppers. She didn't say anything; not that it would have been possible in any event. She stood looking at them. She thumped the monkey wrench gently into the palm of her left hand.

She lifted it, thumped it gently again, lifted it, thumped it, lifted it, thumped it.

They became aware of her. Their eyes followed the small movements of the monkey wrench. They looked at one another, and they looked at Murch's Mom's face. Methodically, without any appearance of undue haste but nevertheless efficiently, they stuffed their mouths with the rest of their whoppers, packed their pockets with french fries, tied their Cokes to their gas tanks with little leather straps and drove away.

Murch's Mom went back to the phone booth. She put down the monkey wrench and picked up the phone. "Hello," she said. "You still there?"

"I'm still here!"

"You don't have to yell," Murch's Mom said. She was being very calm.

"I don't."

"No. But you *have to call that goddam car!*"

The Cadillac breezed past the tomato juice bottle with the instructions in it; milk doesn't come in bottles any more, it comes in plastic cartons. Harrington, on the phone, said to his secretary, "Tell him our client's feeling is he can loan him the seventeen, but he'll need some form of security other than the department store. Tell him, off the record, our client is quite frankly worried about that marital situation of his."

"Yes, sir," said the secretary.

"Should be any second now," Murch said.

Dortmunder twisted around and looked back. No suitcase came falling through the air.

The Cadillac sailed past the Hope exit, over the overpass and on, toward the Delaware Water Gap.

Back at the deserted farmhouse, May and Kelp and Jimmy sat at the card table. "Knock with two," Jimmy said, and spread out his rummy hand.

"Ouch," said Kelp.

"I have to get through to that car!"

138

"When I'm in Washington, we can arrange the meeting with Congressman Henley and then perhaps get a little action."

Murch said, "I think maybe something went wrong."

Dortmunder didn't say anything.

"And if anything else comes up," Harrington said, "you should be able to reach me at home certainly by six o'clock."

"Yes, sir," said the secretary.

Harrington hung up. He said to Maurice, "Nothing's happened yet, eh?"

"No, sir," said the man, who wasn't Maurice at all. That's right; it was the FBI man, Kirby.

"What's that up ahead?" Harrington asked.

"The Delaware Water Gap."

"Oh, really?" Harrington said, and the phone rang. Expecting his secretary to be calling back, he picked it up and said, "Hello?"

Some woman screamed gibberish at him.

"I beg your pardon?"

"What the hell are you doing on the goddam phone!"

"What? Oh, for heaven's sake, it's the kidnapper!"

Kirby slammed on the brakes, and the Caddy slued all over the road. Kirby shouted, "Where? Where?"

"Don't drive like that!" Harrington cried. "Maurice never drives like that!"

"Where's the kidnapper?" Kirby had become calmer again, was driving forward, was looking all around without quite acknowledging the glares of the other drivers passing him, the ones he'd just barely missed when he'd braked so abruptly.

"On the phone," Harrington said. The woman was babbling away on the phone, rancorous and belligerent, and Harrington said, "I *am* sorry. I had no idea. If you'd told me, of course, I would have—"

"Where are you?"

"Where am I? Where you told me to be, on route 80."

"Just crossing the Delaware Water Gap," Harrington said. "Isn't that strange. I've lived so close to it for so many years, and I've just never had occasion to travel this way before. It's really quite—"

"The Delaware *Water* Gap? You're over — you're way the hell and—you went too *far!*"

"I did?"

"You've got to come back. Listen, what you do, you turn around and come back, and I'll go get a road map. Come back, don't drive too fast, stay off the goddam *phone* and I'll call you again."

"All right," Harrington said, and leaned forward to say to Kirby, "We have to go back."

Kirby said, "Do you have a quarter? It's a toll bridge."

Murch's Mom left the phone booth and went over to the Roadrunner. She tossed the wrench on the back seat and went through the glove compartment, looking for a road map, Pennsylvania, New York, Delaware, Connecticut, Utah. Utah? No New Jersey.

There was a Mobil station across the highway from the Burger King. Murch's Mom risked life and limb to run across route 46, get a New Jersey map, and run back again. She studied the map, and then called Harrington again. This was costing a fortune; she'd brought almost ten dollars in change, and it might not be enough.

"Hello?"

"Look," Murch's Mom said. "This is very simple, so just do it and don't screw up."

"I really don't think you have to take that tone with me," Harrington said. "If you'd told me earlier that you meant to contact me on this phone, I would have made sure the line was kept open."

"So you and the cops could set up some sort of trap," Murch's Mom said. "That's what we didn't want."

"The authorities have assured me they will do nothing to endanger—"

"Yeah, yeah. Let's get on with it, all right?"

"Certainly. The ball's in your court."

"The what?"

"You're in charge," Harrington said.

Murch's Mom sighed. "Sure," she said. "Do you have a New Jersey map in the car?"

"I'll check with Maurice. I mean Kirby. I mean Maurice!"

Under the overpass, Murch said, "What the hell do you suppose is going on?"

"I suppose," Dortmunder said, "I suppose I let myself get talked into another Kelp special, that's what I suppose. You notice he isn't here."

"Somebody had to watch the kid."

Dortmunder opened the car door and got out.

"Where you goin'?"

"Look things over," Dortmunder said. He walked along the verge of the road, out from under the overpass and far enough away so he could look up at the highway. He stood there looking at cars go by in both directions. He stood there, trucks and cars going by. The Cadillac went by, in the wrong direction. It was too far away to see the license plate, but it was the right color and it had the whip antenna and that was definitely somebody in a chauffeur's cap at the wheel. And somebody else in the back seat.

Harrington leaned over the New Jersey map. "Yes," he said. "Hackettstown. I see it."

Dortmunder walked back and got into the Mustang. "It just went by the wrong way," he said.

Murch started at him. "The Cadillac?"

"I think something's wrong," Dortmunder said. "That's my personal opinion."

"We better go talk to Mom," Murch said. He started the Mustang and headed south on the county road.

It was ten miles south on the county road to route 46. Then they had to turn left and travel five more miles to get to the Burger King, where they found Murch's Mom sitting morosely in the Roadrunner, eating a whopper. They stopped beside her, and Murch got out and said, "Mom, what—"

Murch's Mom sprayed whopper in all directions. Leaping out of the Roadrunner she cried, "What are you doing *here*?"

Dortmunder said, "They went by the wrong way. What's going on?"

"They're on the way back! I just went through the whole thing with them, they're turning around at the Hackettstown exit. They're on the way!"

"Oh, for Christ's sake," said Dortmunder. "What happened the first time?"

"He was on the phone, I couldn't get through. Will you hurry? He'll get there, somebody else'll pick up the suitcase."

Murch and Dortmunder jumped back into the Mustang and took off. Murch's Mom watched them go, and shook her head. "I swear to God," she said aloud. "I just swear to God."

At the Hackettstown exit, the Cadillac took the off ramp onto county road 517, turned left, took 517 north for about a hundred feet, took the westbound on ramp, and got back up on Interstate 80. Kirby said, "I suppose I can step it up a little bit now."

"I should think so," Harrington said. "We're terribly late, apparently."

Kirby, grinning a little, tipped the chauffeur's cap back on his forehead and hunched a bit over the wheel. His foot became heavy on the accelerator. The Cadillac tyres began to dig in. Harrington, feeling the pressure of the seat back against his spine, began to regret his acquiescence.

State Trooper Hubert L. Duckbundy, driving in an unmarked patrol car which made it possible for him to catch speeders but impossible for rape or robbery victims to contact him in their moment of travail, cruised along at sixty-one, eleven miles an hour above the speed limit,

142

enjoying the fall scenery and waiting for somebody else to do sixty-two, when he suddenly was passed. A silver grey Cadillac, New Jersey plate number WAX 361, chauffeur-driven, was abruptly out front, and going like hell.

Well, well. Trooper Duckbundy accelerated and started the clock. There was nothing more pleasing in the life of a man who brought fifteen thousand, two hundred eighty-seven dollars and ninety cents a year home to his wife and three children than slapping a speeding violation on the operator of a luxury car. *There, you bastard*, was the general theme of the encounter, and for Trooper Duckbundy its satisfactions never palled.

Let's give this one a full mile on the clock, Trooper Duckbundy thought, just to be *sure* he doesn't wiggle out. Ninety-two miles an hour. Oh, my, yes.

But within half a mile the Cadillac's brake lights suddenly went on. Had the driver noticed he was being paced? The Hope exit was near here, maybe the Cadillac meant to leave the Interstate there. If so, Trooper Duckbundy would have to pull him over now, with less than a mile on the clock.

But the Cadillac was more than merely slowing down. Its right directional was on, it was angling over onto the shoulder of the road. Trooper Duckbundy slowed to a crawl, watching the events occurring ahead of him. There's something funny about that, he thought.

The Cadillac stopped. A well-dressed man hopped out of the back seat, picked up a piece of trash from the highway verge, and hopped back into the car again. Trooper Duckbundy's grey Fury II was almost even with the Cadillac when the Cadillac suddenly surged forward again, spraying gravel out behind itself and shouldering itself out onto the highway directly in Trooper Duckbundy's path.

Well, enough is enough. As the Cadillac tore away along the highway, tyres screaming, Trooper Duckbundy switched on the red flasher light mounted on his dashboard, hit the siren, and gave chase.

"Damn," Kirby said, looking in the rearview mirror. They were just passing the off ramp for the Hope exit.

Harrington, struggling against the acceleration to get the message out of the tomato juice bottle, said, "What's wrong?"

"State trooper," Kirby said. "One of those goddam unmarked cars." He braked reluctantly, angling over toward the shoulder again.

Harrington at last got the paper out of the bottle. Then he looked around, saw the flashing red light and saw the siren, and said, "State trooper? But there aren't supposed to be any police around! "

"I'll get rid of him," Kirby said. "No problem."

The Cadillac came to a stop next to the railing of the overpass. The patrol car stopped in front of it, angled across to block it from getting away. The siren was turned off, but the flashing light remained on. Trooper Duckbundy, adjusting his hat and his belt and his trousers and his tie, came walking slowly back to the Cadillac, where Kirby pressed the button that slid the window down. "Going a little fast there, fella," Trooper Duckbundy said.

Kirby flashed his FBI ID card. "It's okay," he said. "A special situation."

Trooper Duckbundy saw that it was an ID card, but that was all. "Licence and registration is all I need," he said. He saw the prosperous-looking fella in the back seat. Mm hm.

"You don't understand," Kirby said. "I'm FBI. This is a special situation here."

"Oh, yeah?" Trooper Duckbundy knew about *this* stuff, too. "And I guess that's a Senator or something in the backseat, is it? Well, let me tell you, we don't like you people thumbing your noses at New Jersey."

"No, you've got it wrong. This—"

"No, I don't have it wrong," Trooper Duckbundy said. "We get a lot of this over on the Turnpike—diplomats, political big shots, going from the UN down to Washington, do eighty, ninety, a hundred miles an hour down through the chemical plants."

"It isn't—"

"You think you got immunity," Trooper Duckbundy said. "Just say a tyre blows at ninety miles an hour, what kind of immunity you got then? And how many innocent people are you endangering, you ever think of that?"

Another police car, this one very well marked indeed, pulled to a stop behind the Cadillac, and the trooper got out to join the action. Harrington said to Kirby, urgently, "They're not supposed to *be* here!" He'd read the note from the tomato juice bottle by now. "This is where we leave the money!"

"Oh, hell," Kirby said.

The second trooper arrived. "We got a problem here?"

"What we have here," Trooper Duckbundy said, "is some sort of politico, a big shot. Think's he's immune to blowouts."

"Is that right?"

"Now look," Kirby said.

The second trooper said to Kirby, "Just a minute there. I'm speaking with the other officer."

Coming like hell, Murch roared toward the intersection of the county road and Interstate 80. As they neared the overpass Dortmunder said, "Isn't that police cars?"

But he'd only had a quick glimpse before the angle was wrong. Murch said, as he braked to a stop under the overpass, "I don't think so. What would they have police cars for?"

"Some sort of trap."

"Be a dumb kind of trap," Murch said, "with police cars." Stopped, he shifted into park but left the engine running. "Better go see if it's there already."

"Right."

Dortmunder got out of the car and went walking over to the other verge of the county road, where the suitcase would land. There wasn't anything there. He walked farther from the overpass, looked up, and saw the Cadillac sandwiched between police cars. The one in back looked like a police car. The one in front was unmarked, but it had a flashing red light revolving behind the windshield.

"Uh huh," Dortmunder said, and walked back to the Mustang and got in next to Murch. "Two police cars," he said. "Also the Cadillac."

Murch shifted into drive.

"No," Dortmunder said. "We can't leave."

"Why not?"

"If it's a trap, they'll spring it when we try to get away. If we stay here after we've seen them, it could be a coincidence, we could be just two guys that stopped to look at a road map. We got a road map?"

Murch shifted into park. "I don't know," he said.

Dortmunder looked in the glove compartment and found a road map. He looked at it. "Illinois?"

"Don't ask me," Murch said. "I just took this car out of a parking lot. The plates I took off it were Jersey, same as the plates I put on."

"A road map is a road map," Dortmunder said. He opened it up, and he and Murch spent some time studying the highways of Illinois.

Up above, Kirby had managed finally to get the word *kidnap* spoken and heard. The second trooper had gone off to radio the barracks for confirmation. Trooper Duckbundy stood frowning at Kirby in a welter of uncertainty. Kirby was angry for more reasons than he could name. And Harrington was hopping up and down on the back seat, saying, "Get them away from here! Get them away!"

"As soon as I can," Kirby said, through gritted teeth. "As soon as I can."

The second trooper came back. "It's okay," he said. He nodded and gave Kirby a Clint Eastwood smile; tough, manly, distanced. "Sorry to horn in," he said.

"Just get the hell away from here," Kirby said.

Both troopers were offended. They went off to their

respective cars, both checking their hats, belts, trousers, and ties. They got into their respective cars, switched off their respective flashing lights, and finally drove the hell away from there.

"At last," Kirby said. "Okay, Mr. Harrington."

"I haven't tried to throw my weight around," Harrington said. "I've done what you people asked, because you're the professionals. But I'm telling you right now that I *do* have influential friends in Washington, and I expect to be chatting with them very soon."

"Yes, sir," said Kirby.

Down below, Dortmunder opened the door of the Mustang and said, "I'll go check it out again. See are they still there."

"Sure," Murch said.

Harrington got out of the Cadillac, carrying the money, and approached the railing. Behind him, Kirby called from the car, "Mr. Harrington!"

He turned around, exasperated beyond endurance. "What now?"

"That's the wrong case," Kirby said.

Harrington looked at the case in his hand, and it was the wrong case. It was his attaché case. "My God," he said. "Good thing I didn't throw that over, it has some rather important documents in it." He hurriedly made the switch in the back seat of the car, getting the suitcase and leaving the attaché case. Then he went back to the railing.

The woman on the phone had emphasized that they shouldn't hang around, they shouldn't be nosy, they should just toss the suitcase over the side and be off. So Harrington just tossed the suitcase over the side and was off. He turned at once, not even looking to see where it landed, and got back into the Cadillac.

As Dortmunder came out from under the overpass, the suitcase hit him on the head and knocked him cold.

"Ouch," said Murch, when he saw that through the windshield. Dortmunder and the suitcase lay side by side

147

next to the blacktop road. Neither of them moved.

Murch shifted into drive, steered the car over there, and shifted back into park. He loaded Dortmunder into the car, tossed the ransom on the back seat, and drove away to the hideout.

23

"I REALLY AM SORRY," Jimmy said. "I'm sure my father didn't do it on purpose."

"Yeah, okay," Dortmunder said. "Just forget it, okay? Ouch!"

"Well, hold still," May told him. "Let me wash the blood off."

They were back at the farmhouse. There was a fire again in the fireplace; that, and the three kerosene lamps, gave the room its illumination. Dortmunder sat in a folding chair while May patted his cut head with a damp cloth, preparatory to putting on it the bandage Murch would soon be bringing back from the drugstore. At the card table, Kelp and Murch's Mom were counting the stacks of bills in the suitcase; Kelp was chortling.

Jimmy said, "My father is really very nonphysical. Really."

"I said forget it."

"It's all right, Jimmy," May said. "Nobody blames your father. It was an accident."

"By golly," Kelp said, "it's all here!"

"It ought to be," Murch's Mom said, "after all we went through."

Murch came in then, revealing a quick view of late afternoon daylight on a rural autumn scene. He closed the door on all that, returning the room to firelit night, and

148

brought a package to May, saying, "No trouble. They're getting to know me in town." He seemed pleased by that.

Kelp said, "Stan, it's all here, every penny."

Murch nodded. "Good," he said, but he didn't sound particularly enthusiastic. Neither success nor failure surprised him; he had the born driver's belief in the task being its own reward. Getting there is half the fun. It isn't whether you win or lose, it's how you play the game.

Murch's Mom said, "You know what I'm getting sick of? I'm getting sick of living in this lousy farmhouse. This place is a landlord's dream come true: no heat, no hot water, no electricity, no phone, and the john doesn't work. I can get the same thing in New York, and be close to the cultural conveniences."

"We'll be leaving tonight," Kelp said. "We unload the—"

"No, we won't," Dortmunder said, and winced while May put the neat white gauze bandage on his forehead.

Kelp was astonished. "We won't? Why not?"

"We'll leave tomorrow morning," Dortmunder said, "and drop the kid in the city."

"Hold still," May told him.

"Well, take it easy," he said.

Kelp said, "Wait a minute. That's not what we do with the kid. In chapter nineteen it says we—"

"I'd hate to tell you," Dortmunder said, "what you can do with chapter nineteen. In fact, with the whole book."

Kelp was astounded and hurt. "How can you argue with it?" he demanded. He gestured toward Jimmy, temporarily out of earshot over by the fireplace, adding a piece of shelf to the fire. "We got the kid, didn't we?" He gestured toward the money on the card table. "We got the cash, didn't we?"

Dortmunder gestured at his new bandage. "I got this, didn't I?"

"That's not the book's fault, you can't blame the—"

"I can blame anybody I damn well want to blame,"

149

Dortmunder said. "That book goes in for too much detail, it makes everything too complicated. You want to know how we're going to give the kid back? I'll tell you how we're going to give the kid back."

Kelp waved his hand in front of himself, then pointed toward Jimmy, who had come back over from the fireplace. "Not in front of the boy."

"It don't matter what he hears," Dortmunder said. "What I got in mind is neat and simple. No school buses, no phone calls, none of that razzmatazz."

"I don't know," Kelp said. His brow was grooved with worry. "I don't think we oughta deviate from the plan," he said. "It's been working out, it really has."

"I don't care," Dortmunder said. "*This* part we do *my* way."

Behind Dortmunder's bandaged head, May waggled a hand at Kelp not to argue. Shrugging, Kelp said, "You're the boss, John, I always said that."

"All right." Dortmunder seemed to shrug his shoulders, to sit a little straighter in the chair. "Now," he said. "We don't let the kid go around here, because that leaves us the whole long run to the city with every cop in New Jersey looking for us. So we take him to New York, and we give him a subway token, and we let him out of the car in midtown. With a token he can't make a phone call to turn the law loose on us right away. All he can do is take a subway or a bus. That gives us time to fade out."

Murch's Mom said, "Why can't we do that tonight? Take him to the city, drop him off, I get to sleep in my own bed, cook a meal, flush a toilet."

Dortmunder said, "Where's the kid go at night? You're gonna leave a kid in midtown at night? Some sex maniac comes along and kills him and *we* get blamed. Tomorrow he can go to his father's office, or he can go up to that place on Central Park West, he can go wherever he wants."

"Sure," Jimmy said. "That sounds fine to me."

150

Dortmunder pointed at him. "I don't need any help from *you*," he said.

May said, "John, the boy was just agreeing with you."

"Well, I don't need it." Dortmunder knew he was being grumpily unfair, and that just made him grumpier. "Where was I?" he said. "Right. We drive him in tomorrow, let him off, get rid of the car, and we all go home. Finished. Done with."

Kelp shook his head. "It just doesn't have the scope of Richard Stark," he said.

"I've had all the scope I need," Dortmunder said. "I've been scoped enough."

"Wonderful," Murch's Mom said. "Another night in the Antarctica Hilton."

Murch said to Dortmunder, "What if we just let him off near his house? Tonight, I mean."

"No," Dortmunder said. "He immediately gets the law on us. We have sixty miles to get to New York, and they know that's where we're headed, and we never make it."

"We can give ourselves an edge," Murch said. "I happened to notice that for the last half mile on the county road to the kid's place there isn't any phone booth at all. No gas stations, no stores, no bars, nothing, just a couple farms, a couple private estates. And you know the way those places are set up for protection from strangers. The kid wouldn't dare just walk in some driveway after dark. He'd get eaten up by a dog first thing, and he knows it."

"That's true," Jimmy said. "On Halloween, when I used to go trick or treating, Maurice had to drive me."

"You keep out of this," Dortmunder told him. To Murch he said, "That still only gives us maybe fifteen minutes head start. In Jersey I can't disappear. In New York I can fade away like that." And he snapped his fingers.

Murch's Mom said to her son, "It's okay, Stan. He's really right, and I can put up with this place one more night. I'm almost getting used to it."

May said, "What about the boy's father?"

Dortmunder said, "What about him?"

"He'll be expecting Jimmy back. I think we should call him, so he won't worry all night."

"You're right," Dortmunder said. "Stan, you and your mom and Andy take the kid to a phone. Let him talk to his father, but make sure he doesn't say too much."

"Oh, good," Jimmy said. "I'll go get my jacket."

They watched the boy trot upstairs. May said, "You know, I'm going to miss that kid."

"Me, too," Murch's Mom said.

"He's an okay kid," Kelp said.

Dortmunder said, "I don't intend to make any big issue of this, but I just want to say one thing. This is not what I had in mind when I decided to go in for a life of crime."

24

EVERY TIME THE phone rang it was for the head FBI man. Harrington kept picking up the receiver and saying hello and some very male voice would invariably say, "Let me talk to Bradford." Bradford was the head FBI man's name.

When the phone rang again at six-fifteen, Harrington said, "Why don't you answer it? It won't be for me."

"Right." The head FBI man was very brisk. He spoke into the phone, nodded (which the other party surely couldn't see, even if he *was* a detective), and smiled in grim satisfaction when he cradled the receiver. "Got them," he said.

Harrington sat up. "You captured them?"

"No, we won't move in till tonight, not till we're sure they're all asleep. We don't want to endanger the boy."

"But you know where they are?"

"Yes." The head FBI man was very pleased with himself and displayed that by flexing his muscles and by making a kind of closed-lip smile in which his mouth became a straight horizontal line with parentheses around it. "They're professional, all right, our kidnappers," he said, "but sooner or later they had to make one mistake, and now they've made it. I was hoping they wouldn't think to get rid of that suitcase." His mouth corners drooped slightly, thoughtfully. "I'm surprised at that oversight," he said, and he sounded almost disappointed that he hadn't been outwitted. "And I'm glad the mechanism didn't get broken when you threw the suitcase over the bridge," he added. "It must have landed on something relatively soft to break its fall."

"And *I'm* glad I didn't know about it beforehand," Harrington said. "It would have made me a nervous wreck."

They'd told him the story after Kirby had brought him back to the house. It seemed they'd "bugged" the suitcase; it now contained a miniaturized radio transmitter, beaming a continuous signal, which could be picked up from as far as a mile and a half away. Three small trucks equipped with radio receivers, always being careful to stay out of sight, had followed that signal from the moment Harrington had entered his Cadillac; they had trailed the suitcase from Harrington to the kidnappers, and then from the kidnappers to their lair. Triangulating on the signal, the three trucks had pinpointed that lair's location, and the kidnappers were now under intense observation.

Harrington said, "Where are they, exactly?"

"Not twenty-five miles from here," the head FBI man said. He was washing his hands together with satisfaction. "They've holed up in an abandoned farmhouse off a county road down toward Hackettstown."

"An abandoned farmhouse? I thought they'd all been snapped up by commuters."

"There's still a few," the head FBI man said. "My

cousin found a deal in Rockland County that—"

The phone rang. Harrington said, "You get that."

"Right." The head FBI man picked up the receiver. "Bradford." He listened, looking very stern. "Right." He listened again. "Keep them under surveillance," he said. "If they leave him, move in. Otherwise, we stick to Plan A." With which he hung up and turned back to Harrington. "They've left the farmhouse," he said. "With the boy. Apparently they're planning to release him now. If they do, naturally we'll move in. If they're simply transferring to another location—"

"You'll stay with Plan A."

The head FBI man frowned. "Exactly," he said, and the phone rang again. "I'll take it," he said, picked up the receiver, and said, "Bradford." Then he looked startled, and said, "Hold on a minute." Cupping his hand over the mouthpiece, he called to the technician dozing over his machinery, "Switch on! Switch on!" To Harrington he stage-whispered, "It's them! Her! She wants to talk to you!"

"Oh," Harrington said. He suddenly felt nervous and faint. He was intensely aware of the technician busily switching on and blinking his eyes to wake up.

"Be very careful," the head FBI man said, and handed Harrington the phone.

Harrington put it to his face as though it were a spider. "Hello?"

The familiar voice said, "Oh, there you are. Who's that Bradford?"

"Um— An FBI man."

"Oh. Sounds like a jerk." (The head FBI man transformed his eyebrows into a bushy straight line low over his eyes.) "Anyway," the kidnapper went on, "I got somebody here to talk to you."

"What?" Harrington felt more and more nervous. Had the kidnappers discovered the transmitter in the suitcase? Were they about to make further demands?

"Hello, Dad?"

"Jimmy! " A flood of warmth suffused him. "By golly, boy, it's good to hear your voice."

"You too, Dad."

"I wasn't looking forward to the ride out tomorrow without you, I can tell you that."

"Well, I'll be there, Dad," Jimmy said.

"I know you will," Harrington said, but when he saw the head FBI man gesturing wildly at him he realized he must be sounding too confident. It wouldn't do to make the kidnappers suspicious at this stage. "That is," he amended, "I was hoping you would."

Jimmy said, "These people want you to know they haven't hurt me, and they're going to let me go in New York tomorrow morning."

"In New York?" Harrington and the head FBI man stared at one another, both startled.

"That's right. Should I come down to your office, or go on up to Dr. Schraubenzieher?"

"Well, I—well—"

"I think I'd rather go to Dr. Schraubenzieher first," Jimmy said. "If that's okay with you."

"Yes, certainly," Harrington said. "After this ordeal, I'm sure you'll want to see him, talk to him."

"It hasn't been much of an ordeal," Jimmy said. "Anyway, it's almost over. Would you call the doctor and change my appointment? Tell him I'd want to get there around noon."

"Yes, I will."

"And I'll call you from his office."

"That's fine," Harrington said.

"Well, I'd better go now," Jimmy said.

"It was good to hear from you," Harrington said. "Um, perhaps we could have lunch. After your appointment."

"Sure," Jimmy said. "I'll be free all afternoon."

"Fine. Good talking to you, son."

"So long, Dad."

Harrington hung up, and the head FBI man said, "Sounds like he's in good shape, considering."

"Well," Harrington said, "he's an intelligent boy, he wouldn't make a lot of trouble."

The head FBI man turned to the technician. "Let's hear that again," he said.

"I think I'd rather not," Harrington said. "If you don't mind."

The head FBI man frowned at him. "Why not?"

"Well, I think I might weep or some such thing," Harrington said, "and I wouldn't want to do that."

25

AT QUARTER TO two in the morning Jimmy used the tweezers to unlock his door again, and went downstairs. A few embers glowed in the fireplace, and one of the kerosene lamps was still lit, standing on the card table like a beacon calling ships in from sea. They'd watched *The Thing* tonight (direction credited to Christian Nyby but more probably the work of producer Howard Hawks, with a screenplay by Charles Lederer, based on *Who Goes There?*, a short story by John W. Campbell, Jr.) and afterward the lady called Mom had insisted that a light be left on. "Otherwise," she'd said, "I won't sleep."

She was asleep, and so was the lady called May, both floating peacefully on their air mattress under mounds of blankets. The three men, called John and Andy and Stan, were presumably asleep in the next room, from which no light at all shone. (They'd been careful, he'd noticed, not to use their last names around him, but they'd been free about using first names, so they were probably all aliases. That's the way professional criminals like these operated; he'd been impressed by their constant references to some previously worked-out master plan, or "book," that they were following through this crime.)

It took less than ten minutes to do what he had to do in the living room, and then he moved swiftly and silently back upstairs, pausing at the top for one last glance down at the sleeping figures in the soft light; they weren't such bad people, really. Probably given psychological scars in their childhoods, and not born into an economic level where treatment could be given at an early age. Understanding, as Dr. Schraubenzieher was fond of pointing out, is the key to nothing except further understanding, but in the last analysis what else is there? All of life is either ignorance or knowledge, there's no third possibility.

Back in the room, he dressed himself as warmly as possible and then once more removed the boards from the window. With his Air France bag over his shoulder, out the window he went, replaced the boards as before, and made his way down the rope.

He had no flashlight with him this time, but on the other hand there was neither wind nor rain to struggle against, and a flashlight could lead to his being discovered before he was ready. The clouded sky made the night almost as dark as last time, but now he had travelled the dirt road unmasked and in daylight, when he'd been taken out to call his father, and he was sure he could find the road in the dark and, once having found it, stay on it by the sense of touch.

This time he went around the house the opposite way, passing the new car Stan and Andy had stolen to replace the Caprice, this one being a Ford Country Squire station wagon. Jimmy squeezed by it, got to the front of the house, found the dirt road by scuffing his feet, and turned right. Though he couldn't see a thing he strode confidently forward, knowing exactly where the road went.

And stopped dead when he heard the cough.

John? Stan? Andy? The women? Had there been any bodies under those mounds of blankets?

No, wait, that's just irrational fear. There's no reason for any member of the gang to come out here and hide in the middle of the night, no reason at all.

Therefore, this must be somebody else.

Even as he was thinking that, someone yawned, very near, on the right. A scratching sound followed, as of someone scratching himself through clothing, and then a voice Jimmy had never heard before said, "God *damn*, this is boring." The volume level was lower than normal, but it was by no means a whisper.

A second voice, speaking more softly than the first, said, "We'll move in soon. As soon as those lights go out."

Turning, Jimmy could see the lines of light at the boarded-up windows. The kerosene lamp seemed much brighter when seen this way.

The first voice, idly complaining, said, "I don't see why we don't go in now and get it over with."

"We don't want anything to happen to the boy," the second voice told him. "We'll wait till they're asleep."

"What if they stay up all night?"

"We'll have to go in before dawn, no matter what."

"I still say," the first voice said, "the easiest thing is let them go tomorrow, follow them with the radio trucks, and pick them up after they let off the kid."

"Too much could go wrong," the second voice said. "They could split up. They could get spooked and kill the kid. And they could still get rid of that suitcase, maybe split the money here and leave it behind. No, Bradford knows what he's doing."

"And I know what I'm doing," the first voice said. "I'm getting goddam bored, that's what I'm doing. Why don't I go peek through the boards again, see if they're still watching television?"

"Just wait here like we were told," the second voice said. "It won't be long now."

At that point, Jimmy turned and headed back for the house, moving as carefully and as silently as he knew how. The two men continued to talk behind him, but he didn't listen any more; he already knew enough. Bradford was the name of the FBI man Mom had talked to on the phone. And there must be some sort of radio transmitter in the suitcase containing the ransom. And now the house was surrounded.

Or was it? These people had apparently done a very solid surveillance on the house, including creeping up on the porch and looking through the window at them watching television. So they must know that the house was completely boarded up, all windows and doors, except the main entrance in front. Isn't that where they would concentrate their forces? In back, where pastureland led to woods, they would have few people or no people at all.

So that's the way they'd have to get out. Thinking it over, Jimmy hurried silently toward the house. He didn't want the gang to get caught, so he'd better warn them pretty fast. Mostly his concern had an ulterior motive—if they were caught it would louse up his own plans—but he also had a kind of reluctant liking for the different members of the gang and didn't want them to get in any trouble. So he hurried.

This time, when he scaled up the rope, he left the boards out of the window. Unlocking the door, hurrying downstairs, he went straight to the suitcase. A transmitter; hmmmmm.

Found it. It looked like a tadpole, a round piece of metal shaped like a nickel, with a tail of wire trailing away from it. A part of the suitcase lining had been pulled out, the transmitter placed behind it, and the lining glued down over it again. An unsuspicious person wouldn't notice it, but a lump like that would never have gotten through customs. Jimmy was surprised nobody in the gang had noticed it.

Holding the transmitter in his hand, he considered his

159

next move. Destroy it? No, they might still have their receivers on, and if the transmitter stopped sending they'd surely attack the house at once. There were still a few shards of shelf stacked up next to the fireplace; he stuffed the thing in among them. Go ahead and transmit now.

How much time did he have? No telling; he hurried across the room to the nearest mound and shook it, whispering, "Wake up! Wake up! "

It was May. She partly sat up, blinking, bewildered, then astonished at seeing Jimmy. "What are *you* doing down here?"

Still whispering, Jimmy said, "There's police outside! "

"What! " May sat upright, shedding blankets, showing she'd gone to sleep in her clothing.

"They're waiting for this light to go out, then they'll move in."

May was waking up fast. Grasping Jimmy's arm she said, "Are you sure?"

"I went outside. I heard them talking."

"You went *outside*?"

"I was going to escape," Jimmy said. "Just to prove a point, I guess. But I heard them, and I came back."

Mom was now sitting up, nearby, and she said, "What's going on?"

May told her, "Jimmy says there's police outside."

"Oh, no! "

"I have a way out," Jimmy told them. "But we have to hurry."

"Yes," May said, suddenly in motion, pulling her shoes on. "Yes yes."

The next five minutes were a frantic scramble. Jimmy had to explain over and over that he'd started to escape, that he'd heard the voices, and that he'd come back to warn the gang. He told them about the kerosene lamp delaying the onslaught, but he didn't mention anything about the transmitter.

May and Mom and Stan and Andy all believed him at

160

once. John was skeptical, for no good reason. "Why'd he come *back*?" he kept asking everybody. "Why'd he come back and *tell* us? Makes no sense."

"You've been fair to me," Jimmy said. "I wanted to be fair to you." He didn't say anything about his own plans for later.

They all wanted to know what his escape route was, but all he'd say was, "Upstairs. And we'd better hurry."

Finally they were all ready to go. The kerosene lamp was left burning, and they all trooped after Jimmy up the stairs. Andy carried the suitcase, Stan carried the portable TV, Mom carried the hibachi, and John carried the flashlight. When Jimmy led the way into his room, John said, "Some day I got to find out how he does that."

Jimmy picked up the Air France bag. "I packed when I was going to escape," he said. "Can I keep it all?"

"Sure," May told him.

"Thanks." To John he said, "We'll have to turn the flashlight off now."

John switched off the flashlight. "I just want to know what we're doing," he said.

Jimmy briefly explained what he had done here, and was greeted with a kind of awed silence. Then he said, "We'll have to go out one at a time. I don't think the rope would be strong enough for more than that."

Andy went first, with the suitcase. Then Stan's Mom went, having trouble squeezing through the space, with her son shoving and holding and helping the best he can. "I can't bring the hibachi," she whispered. "I need both hands on the road."

"I'll bring the damn hibachi," John told her.

Stan helped his mother for the first part down the rope and Andy down below helped her for the last part. Then May went down, and after her, Stan. John said, "You next."

"No, I'll go last," Jimmy said. "I'll fix the boards over

161

the window again, the way I did last time. I already locked the door, while everybody else was going down."

"From the inside?"

"Sure," Jimmy said.

John made some sort of guttural noise in his throat. "All right," he said. "I'll go next."

John went down one-handed, carrying the hibachi. Then Jimmy, the Air France bag over his shoulder again, went out the window for the third and final time. He was very adept by now at replacing the boards, and then he skimmed down the rope and joined the others. "All set," he whispered.

"You want to lead the way?" John asked him. It didn't sound sarcastic, it sounded mostly heavy and fatalistic.

"Not me," Jimmy said. "I don't know what's over there."

"More trouble," John said, and led off.

The six of them marched away from the house in the darkness, off across the scrubby pastureland, following one another mainly by the sound of their footsteps as they tramped through the dry autumn grass. John went first, carrying the flashlight, which he didn't dare switch on. May followed, not carrying anything. Then Jimmy, carrying his Air France bag, Stan's Mom, carrying her hibachi, Stan, carrying his portable TV set, and Andy, carrying the suitcase.

26

At four-twenty A.M., elements of the Federal Bureau of Investigation under the command of Field Agent Leonard Bradford, assisted by elements of the Warren County Sheriff's Department under the command of Sheriff Larch K. Dooley, and elements of the New Jersey State Police under the command of Sergeant Ambrose Rust, broke in the front door of the deserted farmhouse known as the Pootey place, Hezakiah Township, Lot 19, Block 47, and shouted, "Hands up!"

And found the place empty.

Agent Bradford, entering with the second wave, announced, "They're in here someplace! Tear it apart."

They tore it apart. State troopers, sheriff's deputies, and Federal agents reported to Bradford in streams, and all of the reports were discouraging. There was no one in the building. A second-floor room, furnished for a child and locked from the outside, was empty. Air mattresses, blankets, food, folding chairs, and other indicators indicated that the fugitives actually had been in this building—thus confirming the eyewitness report of Agent Wilson, who had peeked in and seen them all watching television—but they sure weren't here now.

Nor, unfortunately, was there any way for them to have left. Every door and every window in the place was solidly boarded up, with the single exception of the front door, which had been under constant surveillance since late yesterday afternoon. There were no tunnels in the basement, no secret passages, no hidden rooms. They were not here, and it was not possible for them to have left.

And what made it worse, the radio trucks claimed they were still here. The three trucks were out roaming the world, triangulating and triangulating and triangulating, and every damn time the three lines crossed at the exact same spot on the map. This spot.

The gang wasn't here. The child wasn't here. The suitcase wasn't here. But the gang and the child could not have left, and the radio trucks insisted the suitcase *was* here.

By dawn's early light, Agent Bradford stood on the sagging front porch and watched his demoralized men wandering around that field out there, looking for clues. Sergeant Ambrose Rust of the New Jersey Police came out of the house, after one last head-scratching inspection, and said, "Well, Mr. Bradford, what do we do now?"

"I don't know about you, Sergeant," Agent Bradford said, "but I'm going to start looking for somebody to pin this on."

27

IN THE DEEP dark woods they huddled around the television set, for warmth as much as for entertainment. The movie now was *Captain Blood*, Errol Flynn's first picture, directed by Michael Curtiz, best known for *Casablanca*. Jimmy was pointing out to an uncaring audience how the obsessive close-ups of Flynn from a low-angle camera made him separate from and above the surrounding action when Kelp came blundering back through the woods to say, "Well, I finally found something. It wasn't easy out here, let me tell you."

It was now shortly after dawn; *Captain Blood* would soon be giving way to *Sunrise Semester*. They had spent over an hour heading away from the house, first across open fields, then through woods, then across a county road and a ploughed field and more woods until they'd felt secure enough to stop. Another county road was ahead of them; while the rest retired deeper into the woods to hide and watch television, Kelp had gone off to find them transportation, a vehicle to get them to New York.

And now Kelp was back. Slowly Dortmunder rose, clutching his back. He had found and fixed the leak in his air mattress, but the patch had popped during the night and he'd awakened stiff as a board again. Sitting around on the cold ground late at night hadn't helped much, so that by now the movie character he resembled was no

164

longer Frankenstein's Monster but the Tin Woodman before he's been oiled.

"Oh, to be home," Murch's Mom said. "Home in my own warm bed."

Jimmy said, "Can't we watch the finish? It's really well done."

"I'm almost willing," Dortmunder said. "I'd like to see something well done."

"Like a steak," Murch said.

May said, "Don't talk about food."

They turned off the TV, over Jimmy's protests, and all trailed after Kelp through the woods and out to the county road, where they found a Ford Econoline van waiting for them. Colored dark green, it had lettering on the side doors that read BUXTON J. LOWERING, D. V. M.

Dortmunder said, "What's this?"

"The only vehicle I could find," Kelp said, "that didn't have dogs or barbed wire in the way of me getting to it. People are very mistrustful out here, don't believe any of that stuff about the gullible hicks."

"D. V. M.," May read. "That's some kind of doctor, isn't it?"

"Even out here," Murch said, "he steals doctors' cars."

"Doctor of Veterinary Medicine," Jimmy said.

Dortmunder looked at Kelp. "A vet?"

"It's all I could find," Kelp insisted. "*You* go look."

"No," Dortmunder said. "It's okay. Stan, you and your Mom ride up front. The rest of us'll get in back. And Stan?"

"Mm?"

"Just get us to the city, okay?"

"Sure," Murch said. "Why not?"

Kelp opened the rear doors of the van, and they started to climb in. Wistfully May said, "And we were going back in a Country Squire. I was really looking forward to that."

Most of the interior was taken up by a large cage. They had to get into the cage, there being no place else to sit down, and try to get comfortable on the crisscross metal bars of the cage floor. Jimmy sat on his Air France bag, May sat on the suitcase, and Kelp tried sitting on the TV set. When that didn't work he tried the hibachi, which also didn't work. Dortmunder, past caring, simply sat down on the floor.

Murch turned and called, "All set back there?"

"Just wonderful," May said.

Murch started them forward. The drive wasn't as bumpy as it might have been.

"Andy," Dortmunder said.

"Uh huh?"

"The next time you have an idea," Dortmunder said, "if you come to me with it, I'll bite your nose off."

"Now what?" Kelp was aggrieved again. "Doggone it, this thing's working out isn't it? We're making thirty thousand apiece out of it, aren't we?"

"I'm just saying," Dortmunder said.

"I don't see how you can complain."

"I'm complaining anyway," Dortmunder said. "And I'm also warning you."

"Boy. Some people are just never satisfied."

May said, "What's that smell?"

"Dog," Jimmy said.

"Sick dog," Dortmunder said.

"I suppose that's my fault, too," Kelp said.

Nobody said anything.

28

"I USED TO like dogs," May said. "In fact, I had one once."

"Lincoln Tunnel coming up," Murch called to them.

"That's not all that's coming up," May said.

They'd been in this truck for nearly two hours, excep

for three pauses at rest stops along route 80, when they would all get out and do a lot of breathing. Dortmunder, whose stiffness wasn't being helped by sitting on a cage floor and leaning his back against a cage wall, would simply stand behind the truck during the rest stops, hanging there like an elm tree struck by the blight, but the others would all walk around, inhaling and limbering up.

"It'll be over soon," Kelp said, but not with his usual sparkle. He'd cut out the sparkle about an hour ago, when after one optimistic remark he'd made Dortmunder had given him a flat look and had started thumping his right fist into his left palm. Now, Kelp too seemed beaten by events, even if only temporarily.

Lincoln Tunnel. Murch paid the toll, and they drove through, following a slow-moving, belching tractor-trailer bringing—if the back doors could be believed—pork fat to an anxious city.

Out the other side, Murch scooted the van around the tractor-trailer and headed up Dyer Avenue to Forty-second Street, where a red light stopped him. "Where to?" he called back.

"Out," Dortmunder said.

Kelp said, "Don't we have to let the kid off first?"

"That's right," Dortmunder said.

May called to Murch, "Stop at Eighth Avenue. He can take the subway there, up to Central Park West."

"Right."

Jimmy had been half-dozing, sitting on his Air France bag and leaning back against May's side. Now she jostled his shoulder, saying, "Here we are, Jimmy. New York."

"Mm?" The boy sat up, blinking. When he stretched, his bones cracked like tree limbs. "Boy, what a trip," he said.

Murch drove to Eighth Avenue and stopped. May gave the boy a token, and Kelp opened the rear door for him. Carrying his bag, he climbed awkwardly out onto the street. (In some places this might have caused comment,

167

but at Eighth Avenue and Forty-second Street in New York City a twelve-year-old boy with an Air France ba climbing out of the back of a veterinarian's truck at eight thirty on a Friday morning was the closest thing to nor mality that had happened there in six years.)

"So long, Jimmy," May called, and waved to him.

"So long, everybody," Jimmy said, waving to them al through the open door of the truck. "Don't feel bad," h said, and turned away.

Kelp pulled the door shut, and Murch drove them on "How much farther?" he asked.

"Turn down Seventh," Dortmunder said, "and park a soon as you can."

Kelp was frowning. He said, " 'Don't feel bad'? Wha did he mean, 'Don't feel bad'?"

May said, "I suppose because we're all separating now We kind of got close there, after all, and he *did* warn u about the police."

Kelp continued to frown. "It doesn't feel right," he said.

Dortmunder looked at him. "What's up?"

"The kid said, 'Don't feel bad.' Why would he—?"

Kelp blinked. Dortmunder looked at him. The two c them swivelled their heads and looked at the suitcase Ma was sitting on. May said, "What's the mat—?" Then sh too looked down at the suitcase. "Oh, no," she said.

"Oh, no," Kelp said.

"Open it," Dortmunder said.

Murch, stopping for the red light at Seventh Avenue called, "What's going on back there?"

They were all on their knees now around the suitcase May was releasing the catches. She was opening it. The were looking in at two pieces of broken shelf, for weigh and several pieces of small-size clothing, to keep the board from rattling around.

"He pulled a switch on us," Kelp said.

Dortmunder yelled at Murch, "Circle the block! G that kid back!"

The light was green. Murch tore the Econoline around the corner, down to Forty-first Street, and made the next right turn on the yellow.

"Here's something else," May said, and took from the suitcase a small package wrapped in brown paper.

Murch, driving like hell, yelled back, "What's happening?"

"He pulled a switch on us," Kelp yelled. "He left us his laundry!"

May had opened the package. Inside the brown paper was a stack of bills. "There's a note here," May said, and read it aloud while Kelp counted the bills. "Dear friends. Thank you for everything you've done for me. Let this be a small token of my esteem. I know you're too smart to come after me again, so this must be farewell. Kindest regards, Jimmy."

"There's a thousand bucks here," Kelp said.

"Two hundred apiece," Dortmunder said. "We just made two hundred dollars."

"Here we are," Murch said, and braked to a stop at Eighth Avenue and Forty-second Street.

Jimmy was gone.

29

September 29

Mr. John Donald Riley
27 West 45th St.
New York, N. Y. 10036

Dear John:

I know I promised you I'd never get involved in a lawsuit again, but I think this just might be the exception to the rule. My friend Hal out on the coast tells me he's seen a rough cut of a movie called *Kid Stuff* that is a direct steal from my book *Child Heist*, except it's played for laughs. Now, it's bad enough to steal from me, but to make fun of me at the same time is even worse.

Hal says the thing is a low-budget no-name-star quickie done here in the east, produced and written and directed by somebody named James Hurley Harrington. I don't know who this Harrington is, he's never done anything else, but he's obviously a crook.

I'm told the distribution deal is being worked out with either Columbia or MGM. Maybe the best way to approach it is through them instead of going after this Harrington direct. But you're the lawyer, so I'll leave that up to you. Hal tells me there's no question, it's an open-and-shut case.

Say hello to Maribelle and the kids.

Yours,
Richard Stark

October 7

Mr. Richard Stark
73 Cedar Walk
Monequois, NJ 07826

Dear Dick:

Enclosed find a tax form from England to be filled out. It's the usual form telling them you're an American citizen and have not lived in their territory in the last eighteen months. You could send it on to the publisher direct.

I've looked into the situation re *Kid Stuff*, and I'm afraid the story there is more complicated than it might seem at first blush. James Hurley Harrington, to begin with, is a thirteen-year-old boy, apparently a child genius of some kind. The story I get, and I do believe I have this on good authority, is that Harrington himself was kidnapped just about a year ago, the ransom was paid, and the boy was released unharmed. His father is well off, and has apparently put up the hundred and fifty thousand or so that it took to make the picture.

It seems to me, Dick, there's no question but that the kidnappers used your book in abducting the Harrington boy However, Harrington himself has used only the events which in fact happened to him, and as you know factual events cannot be copyrighted. If there is an infringement of copyright here, and I don't see how there can help but be, I doubt you could make a case against anyone but the kidnappers. And, unfortunately, no one knows who they are.

I understand from my own sources, by the way, that it's quite a funny little movie.

Sincerely,
John Donald Riley

30

DORTMUNDER COULD NEVER get used to the feeling of riding in the cab of a tractor-trailer when there wasn't any trailer hooked on the back. This big loud red engine, snorting diesel fumes out of a pipe just above his window, growling through all the gears, struggling like it was pulling a building along behind itself, and when you turn around and look back there's nothing there. Just the growling cab and himself sitting up high on the passenger's side while Stan Murch did the driving. For some reason, this cab-without-trailer experience always made Dortmunder feel as though he were tilting forward, as though he were about to fall off a cliff. He kept his feet planted on the floor and his back pressed against the seat.

"There's Kelp," Murch said.

Dortmunder squinted. "I see him," he said.

It had taken a long time for Dortmunder to be willing to see Kelp again—almost a year. And a couple of months after that before he'd work with him any more. He still wouldn't have anything to do with any big stuff Kelp might bring around, but he was grudgingly willing now to join in with Kelp on the occasional burglary or, like tonight, the occasional hijacking.

It was nine o'clock in the evening, and this space under the West Side Highway along the piers was lined with trailers. Some were empty, waiting to be loaded tomorrow morning with goods coming in by ship. Others were full, waiting to be off-loaded tomorrow morning with their goods going *into* ships. Almost all of them were trailers only, without cabs.

This was the best time of day to hit this area. Late enough for the workmen all to have gone home, but not so late than any passing patrol car would get suspicious. Hook their cab onto a trailer, drive down to Brooklyn, turn it over to their contact there, take their money, go home.

But not just any trailer. It had to be a trailer with useful goods in it. Like the one tonight. Kelp claimed to have learned about a trailer full of television sets. If he was right, it was rent money and then some.

Murch pulled to a stop next to where Kelp was loitering. Kelp had been prepared to fade away between the trailers if anybody else had come along, but now he stepped boldly out and said, "Hiya," as Dortmunder climbed down from the cab.

"Hello," Dortmunder said. They had an agreement; they were polite, even friendly with one another, but neither of them ever mentioned the past. It had been a year and a half since the kidnapping fiasco and they both knew that Dortmunder still had a tantrum left in him on that one and that the tantrum, if it did burst, would have to burst on Kelp's head. So neither of them talked about yesterday, or permitted any reminder of the past.

172

"It's this one," Kelp said, gesturing to a ratty-looking trailer with a lot of dents on it.

Dortmunder looked at it, and the trailer just didn't give the impression of being full of valuable things. He said, "You sure?"

"Positive."

"Yeah," Dortmunder said, and he did not say, *You've been positive before.* What he did, he walked down to the back of the trailer, saying, "Let's just double-check."

Kelp, following him down between the trailers, said, "I don't think maybe we ought to—"

Dortmunder threw the lever and opened the rear door.

The alarm made an awful sound, it went right through your head like a science-fiction ray gun. "Shit," Dortmunder said. Through the open door, streetlight glare reflected off white cartons with the letters *TV* on them. "Shit again," Dortmunder said.

Kelp was already running, and now Dortmunder followed him. Murch was boiling out of the stolen cab, and all three men ran across Twelfth Avenue and down into the warren of side streets known as the West Village. After two blocks they slowed to a walk, and then strolled on eastward toward Greenwich Village, ignoring the propositions of the homosexuals who hung out in this area at night.

It took Dortmunder four blocks to build himself up to it but finally, gritting his teeth, he turned toward Kelp and said, "I'm sorry."

"It's okay," Kelp said. "Could have happened to anybody." He was so glad that for once he couldn't be blamed for what had happened that he didn't even mind the loss of the TV sets.

They walked on a bit farther, reaching the relatively bright lights of Sheridan Square, where they stopped again and Murch said, "So now what?"

"Look," Kelp said. "We're done so early, why don't we grab a movie? Stop off, pick up May, go to a movie."

"A movie," Dortmunder said.

"Sure. Maybe a nice comedy, take our minds off our troubles. There's a new one out called *Kid Stuff*, supposed to be pretty funny. Whadaya say?"

"Sure," Murch said.

Dortmunder shrugged. "What can it hurt," he said.